Be happy, today may be your birthday!

Soup of the Day

Served with your choice of crustless bread
and creamy butter!

Main Course

Salmon Fillet

Sprinkled with finely chopped parsley, effortlessly
courted and wooed by baby potatoes and vegetables.
Served with lemon or lime flavoured rice!

Dessert

Your favourite flavour ice cream with marshmallows!
A bowl of sweet and colourful delights!

Dinner at Ted's
(An Olive Branch)

Edward, St. David's

For

My three good buddies:

Mum, Dad and Aunt Grace.

My dear departed brother, David

and

George Reed, my English teacher at Ardvreck.

In gratitude!

Published by Jessie Grace Publishing
Second Edition

Copyright © Edward, St. David's 2023

Edward, St. David's has asserted his right under the
Copyright, Designs and Patents Act, 1988, to be identified
as the author of this work.

First Edition Paperback ISBN: 978-1-7391187-0-9
First Edition eBook ISBN: 978-1-7391187-1-6

Second Edition Paperback ISBN: 978-1-7391187-2-3
Second Edition eBook ISBN: 978-1-7391187-3-0

Cover design and typeset by SpiffingCovers

www.edwardstdavids.com

Contents

For the regretful
Those who sit on a plain wooden chair
Alone in the vastness

This story is a key
An odd looking and very costly key
And that key is now yours

Prologue

She could hardly hear herself laugh, and who could blame her?

She could hardly hear her own childish thoughts, and who could blame her?

For Saturday it was, it truly was! The eight-year-old girl, a once reluctant prisoner of the need to sleep, woke and sprang-bounced out of bed, running through to jump on her dozing parents, creating a world of giggling, flying duvet confusion and energy!

"Wake up Lazy Bones!" she shouted as the two grown-ups under said duvet fought desperately to find the fabled land of Awakeness. Both knew they would be held to their word to go to the park, given the night before.

"Ok ok *ok!!* It must be Saturday then, I reckon," said Mum. Her reluctance was only surface. Inwardly these moments were life's blood itself. Pure scarlet oxygen joy! There was a growl from under the duvet.

"Who's waking me up? I'll gobble up that rascal for my breakfast!!"

Dad basically fell out of his side, still growling. The daughter shrieked then laughed as she ran…with Dad in not so hot pursuit.

***

Saturday breakfast was always such fun! Talk of plans and promises, both now and future, saturated in anticipation, ricocheted off kitchen surfaces. Buying some new toy after the park? *Sure!* Joining ballet class on Wednesday? *What else!* Planning a holiday with all the in-laws? *Bring it on!* Ask and ye shall indeed receive! Cereals were guzzled as the aroma of toast gave its olfactory siren call. To be included, to be one of *this* crowd, to be an "Insider" and join *this* particular congregation required birth into such and, if that applied to *you*, boy, you were *in!*

This was following the instruction manual of joy unspeakable to the letter!

This was life in the "In" lane!

***

The visit to the park did just what it said on the tin! Laughter from about ten or so well satisfied children mostly hid the sounds of creaky swings and squeaky roundabouts. Some parents were in the play area also, pushing those swings; others just sat on the side benches and waved to their child every five seconds. No awkward silences here between parents as only shallow pleasantries were called for, suiting shyer adults just fine. Some huddled on the benches and were firmly in "gossip" mode; all but ignoring their child. The only words spoken by any child were

"Faster!" and "Again, again!" Did anyone even notice the firm breeze rustling spring leaves? No matter but it was there anyway! The sun was there also, putting ice cream at the forefront of everyone's thoughts. For all present, whether adult or child, whether caring or indifferent, whether gossiping or shy, this was life in the "Fun" lane!

Our eight-year-old friend was there of course with a now fully awake Mum and Dad.

"I see you, darling, I see you!" shouted Mum, waving. The little girl was very fortunate as her parents were neither shy nor prone to public gossip, they were just actual "parents". Dad pushed more as requested, higher and higher and again and again and again.

So this just went on and on. As the girl swung, she noticed her mother standing up and making a beckoning gesture to her father.

"Just a moment, sweetheart, I'll be back in a sec!" he said with one final great big push to keep momentum going. He left the play area and spoke briefly to Mother then the two of them walked, rather plainly and morbidly, off and out of sight. This was witnessed by the girl, who let momentum cease, alighting the swing in mounting panic, running out of the play area.

"Daddy, Daddy, *DADDY!!!*" with eyes welling up, breathing beyond rapid. She stood nearly fainting with apparent abandonment, a feeling hitherto not encountered, sweeping around her. Reaching the top of a slight rise, she looked around frantically. Mum

3

and Dad were her world and what is there if you have no world? Senses were focused to the hilt now, beyond what any child should be experiencing. Suddenly the sought after were spotted and, *WHOOSH*, the relief! Her parents were leaving a building just twenty yards away that the girl had never noticed before; never noticed not out of play intent but because the building, which was of the most boring, clinical design, had simply not *been* there before.

Wait, what was this? Mum was in a wheelchair and terrifically deep in thought, or at least her frown gave that impression. As if part of some procession, Dad pushed her the absurdly short distance from the clinic entrance to the car. He huddled Mum ever so tenderly from chair to car. The girl - their daughter - was about to run towards them when she heard a loud *CLANK* of a noise from behind. She looked to see one of the other parents closing the play area gate from within. She ran down the slight incline to see that the play area fence was now made out of savage barbed wire mingled thoroughly with black thorns. The gate had disappeared and this cruel new barrier of barbs cut off the play area from all outsiders. To salten the shock, boisterous play continued and waving, pushing, gossiping parents continued.

And what was better for the girl to see: that just over the crest, her parents had driven away without her or the sight of the park she would never enter again? She stood in a heat haze of bewilderment for a trice then collapsed to the ground. No one noticed any of this, absolutely no one.

*** *** ***

The bride, surrounded by her ladies, stood before the full-length mirror.

A clamour of pealing church bells argued over who would get to proclaim the glad tidings of her happy today! With an auburn-haired beauty adorned in undulating and luxuriant silk folds with lace hemming standing before it, the mirror was afraid to even attempt a reflection. For today, yes, just today, for these few hours, cursed to be so very fleeting, this Queen was the only piece on the chessboard. Who dare draw near this lady and proclaim their own beauty? Even an angel would take a step back.

"Is this *me?* I mean, really really *me?*" said Auburn Worthy.

"Sure is, honey!" said Best Friend.

"Say that again!" said our bride. Her sighing, rolling-eyed best buddy was joined by the four other ladies in the room, all chanting in unison:

"*Sure is, honey!*" The bride covered her face and started to cry.

"*What!* Now cut that out or it's all off you rascal!" said Best Friend, putting an arm round her with a squeeze. "It's because of you that we've flown thousands of miles to be here!" And, of course, Best Friend was right, it *was* because of her...

***

"I'll take that as a '*Yes*' then shall I?" he said as he caught Auburn Fainting in mid swoon, seconds after his proposal of marriage. She lay flopped in his arms for a few seconds before slowly awakening to handsome ecstasy. She squeezed his neck and sobbed her line bang on cue:

"Yes, yes, yes, yes, yes!"

***

They had met when the groom visited her country on a working holiday with a few friends. He had seen her and remarked that, because of her hair colour, she probably had Scottish ancestry. This possibility, and, of course, that Scottish accent, had piqued her interest and thrilled her out of the mundane and into the realms of romantic possibilities. His "everything" just stole her clean away. Oh please, do not let this ever ever end!

A short while and her heart had emigrated utterly to his. She now pondered on romantic clichés that she had heard, and maybe even scoffed at, all her life and realised just why those clichés were such, for, as she looked down, she saw her path was now paved with them. And where on Earth had everyone disappeared to? Were she and her love the only two people God had ever *made?* Oh please, I ask again, do not let this ever *ever* end!

So she visited his homeland and gentle adventure followed gentle adventure. Now they walked towards a fork in the river behind Doune Castle. Hands were held but naught was spoken as both were too dumbstruck at their good fortune in finding each other. Only God and the birds in the trees were considered worthy to witness the final destination of love's journey. This was every romance novel ever written; both the cheap and the monumental; pulped and injected straight into your soul. Now he turned to face the only piece on that chessboard.

So he took her hand and knelt…

Knelt and cried and asked…

Asked this particular Queen for her heart.

One moment before fainting, Auburn Fulfilled, one of the luckiest girls that ever lived, had but one thought: *"Oh please please please, I ask thee thrice; do not let this ever, ever end!"*

***

"Well c'mon honey, there's a Rolls-Royce waiting outside with your name on it!" said Best Friend. Final sprays of whatever women spray at this time. White rustling chaos and final, head-clashing looks in the mirror then the ladies in waiting rushed out of the room, squealing and giggling, leaving Auburn Heart Thumping alone with her mother. An obligatory moment for a final word from mother to daughter, perhaps?

Mother took out a little plastic container from her handbag as Auburn Intrigued looked on. A pill box this was. Just a tiny plastic pill box. No harm, surely.

"Mother, are you alright?" No answer as a pill was tipped into Mother's hand and a glass of water was reached for off the dressing table.

"*Mother, are you ok?*" Still no answer as the pill was downed with a few sips.

"*Mother, tell me, what's wrong?*" Mother's head had been bowed somewhat, her wide-brimmed wedding hat hiding her face well. She began sobbing a little then looked up at her daughter.

"Darling, oh darling, I am so very very sorry. I really am." She placed the pill box on the dresser and Auburn Shocked could clearly see it said:

ABORTION PILL

Then Auburn Betrayed closed her eyes and bowed her head then collapsed in a heap.

Then the Queen, now deposed and with her army scattered, fell and lay alone on the chessboard, her chequered kingdom in ruins.

Then Auburn Defeated, who had swooned in the arms of her love, was lowered gently onto the summer grass at the fork in the river by the same. He stood and looked straight ahead, then, without a care in the world, turned and walked away to another life.

He had no memories of her now.

*** *** ***

"OK…OK…I'm *ready* already!"

Teri-An applied just that last bit of lipstick in the same way she had applied just that last bit of lipstick thirty seconds earlier. She and her husband were throwing a Christmas party. This was no small undertaking as many people attended their parties. Teri-An was a people magnet due to her loving and selfless personality. Lucky Husband knew exactly how lucky he was and sometimes cried in secret because Teri-An was his all and he felt unworthy. A firm knock on the bathroom door.

"OK…I'm coming," as she applied just that last bit of lipstick.

"I can see the first car arriving," said Lucky Husband. Teri-An threw the bathroom door open with a *"ta-daa!"* and a twirl. She twirled and twirled right into Lucky Husband's arms. There was that sense of unworthiness again.

"Time for a dance, you most *handsome man?"* as she gently stroked his cheek.

"Look Teri…"

"A quickstep then! We can fit one in, surely!"

"Listen, there's the doorbell!" said Panicking Husband.

"Party Pooper!" she replied, poking his middle-aged belly a few times, saying *"cha cha cha!"* before grabbing his hand and dragging him downstairs.

***

There was no "mwah mwah" with Teri-An. Everyone got a tight – almost *too* tight – hug and several pecks on their cheek. Had they turned on the spot and gone home right at that point they would have been more than happy. With front-of-house skills already installed from birth that automatically updated as she slept, Teri-An could throw a blistering party in a cemetery. Life one click too loud sometimes, one click too trusting sometimes and one click too prone to hurt feelings sometimes, this was the portrait called Teri-An. She had been given the chance to live and guzzled it in a gulp, and, if *she* was going to live, she was going to take as many people with her as she could!

***

The neighbours couldn't complain about the noise because every neighbour was at the party! Galloping festivities these were! At your usual party, about 30% to 50% of attendees will not even be recognised by the hosts. Most invitees brought something such as a bottle of wine, which they opened and finished off themselves, or home-made food, which they opened and then ate themselves. "Mr Flirt", "Mr Always in the Kitchen" and "Mrs Mutton Dressed as Lamb" were there, as they are at anyone's party. How they got hold of an invite is anyone's guess. But, to be honest, whatever quirky people with their quirky ways were there, it all added to the fun. What is a party without them, after all?

Oh, just how *happy* Teri-An was! She had a part-time job as a waitress which she loved as it gave her benevolent nature full vent and came in so handy for occasions such as this one. She loved cheery music and eighties catchy pop was her favourite. This was convenient as it masked the sound of somebody throwing up in the downstairs toilet. The main stampede of guests had arrived and now the odd latecomers arrived in dribs and drabs.

To wander among the throng and eves drop as you pass; conversations sang from heart cloisters that were freed for a while from the drudge of life.

"You know, Teri honey, your parties are worth ten times what I pay the babysitter!"

"That's great to hear! I'd get out more myself but no one will babysit my husband," replied Teri-An.

"Ouch, I heard that!" said Lucky Husband.

"Oh c'mere," said Teri-An as she hugged his neck, "I would never go *anywhere* without you, would I schnookums?!"

"No," he replied "cause it's part of your parole conditions!" as he slapped her behind.

***

As the mingling continued, Teri-An noticed two solitary figures standing off to one side. She had glimpsed them on and off during the revelry. Silent figures they were, both dressed in white; a mature-looking man and a young woman. They had stood rooted to the spot not long after suddenly appearing, it would seem, in the room. No one had spoken to them nor they to each other but they had simply stood staring blankly at Teri-An. A natural space surrounded them that no one seemed to enter.

Teri-An felt, as she regarded them, a connection between her destiny and theirs. Why though, in the very midst of happiness, should they appear? Why come to a party only to shun participation on all levels? Just why? Their eyes locked with hers and she walked towards them. As she drew closer she saw the man was a doctor in a white doctor's coat with a stethoscope draped round his neck. The young woman was in a nurse's uniform. All sound faded and faded with each step of approach till the three stood face to face in silence.

"You cannot be here, Teri-An," said the doctor.

"Why?" asked Teri-An, very calmly.

"Because of something someone did many years ago. I am sorry."

"We are truly sorry," said the young nurse.

Teri-An stared at them both for what seemed like an age, then extreme dizziness swept over her. She turned and stumbled through the still ongoing party, staggering and colliding into guests who took no notice. The music sounded weird now. She saw her husband chatting and made towards him but fell on to a table of food which toppled over, spilling sandwiches and empty wine glasses everywhere with a crash, and still no one noticed or looked her way. With Herculean effort, Teri-An struggled to her feet one last time and cried, "Well help me someone!", but the world as she knew it was becoming lost to her.

So Teri-An – the life of the party – had herself become death. She slammed into the living room wall then fell to the floor with a pathetic moan. No one, not one single person, noticed this or reacted. The party stopped abruptly, not by human design but by something else. All music ended, all chatter ended. The doctor and nurse walked out of the room, followed by everyone else in utter silence, just the sound of morbid movement leaving the building. No one spoke of Teri-An because no one knew anyone *called* Teri-An.

***

The odds of *this* happening were incredible!

But, as life would have it, these things really do happen sometimes. After all, *somebody* always wins the lottery, don't they?! This particular jackpot was one of timing, location and weather.

The university building was simply splendid. A seat of learning for nearly a thousand years, it was hard, from many angles, to differentiate it from a medieval fortress built to intimidate enemies. No doubt many a nervous scholar, in centuries gone by, trod gingerly through its gates the first time they entered; a tradition that very likely held to this day.

And, of course, universities are places of thronging, aren't they? The road to academic fulfilment has many avenues, and, between lectures, a veritable dam burst of the knowledge-seeking flood cloisters, hallways and cafeterias. No shortage of life blood flows through the nooks and crannies of this place! This symbiotic set up between student and university obviously works – it's a thousand years old, remember!

Add a near cloudless day to this and those intimidating fangs begin to be pulled, leaving the building only in possession of its architectural beauty. Trembling doth retreat and bow before admiration and joy! Friezes, thrown into sharp relief, are released by sunbeams from their stone beds and dance for a while; the craftsmen who carved them smiling from afar off in time. Every Christmas the natural stone surroundings are put to good use by carols that echo sweetly and endlessly as only true praise can. Come now, is the real purpose of this building not yet apparent unto you? It was not built to cause distress and intimidate as you first thought, but to bless and improve!

Today is Graduation Day no less! Did we talk of thronging? It is here! Did we mention joy bordering on dancing? See, it is here also! Bright is this day on many levels for it is the finishing line of a race, the completion of an arduous course, the birthplace of careers and the final bestowing of promised rewards!

The young and newly qualified doctor leaned in very close to her grandmother for a selfie. These moments are why people are born, surely.

"Smile, Grandma, smile!"

"I've done little else since the day you were born, darling!" replied Grandma.

The click sound effect "clicked" on Doctor Granddaughter's phone and the moment went down in family history.

"Now one of me with you and Granddad!"

"Anything you say, Doctor, I feel better already!"

The three of them huddled and there was that click sound effect again. Granddad magically produced something from out of his pocket.

"Happy Anniversary to the prettiest girl I ever saw!" he said as he handed Grandma Taken Aback a small box that could only contain jewellery of some sort. Before Grandma could react, he pulled another similar box from his other pocket.

"And Happy Birthday to you!" For yes, many many years before this day dawned, Granddad and Grandma had married on her birthday! The coincidence had been a real talking point throughout their many years of marriage. When somebody, somewhere, decided that Graduation Day would be on this exact date, they brought a lot of happy planets into joyous conjunction; after all, *somebody* wins the lottery, don't they?

"Oh, please now, honey, we agreed not to steal someone's thunder, didn't we?" protested Grandma.

"Nonsense, this is your day too! The coincidence is too great not to celebrate!"

"I know, honey, but..." Her protest was abruptly ended by Granddad planting a sloppy kiss on her lips.

She turned her head away and waved her hand as if shooing away a fly.

"Still blushing after all these years!" said Granddad.

"With you around, I have little choice!" she replied.

This was harvest time for the elderly pair. They had sat and watched the near magical sight of each generation pulling the next out of a top hat. Grandma had lain in bed each and every night, sometimes in moonlight and sometimes not, and reflected on the self-perpetuating human race. She had been so lucky to live so long to see the births of people who had simply not existed before, with personalities that had simply not existed before, and know that they were blood related. It had been worth the wait, it really had. Her family were her all...and that was that.

And so the afternoon just kept up the pace on the immaculately mown, sun-bathed university grounds. Tables had been laid out, each with a parasol and jug filled with ice and soft drinks. Many photos were taken by our family: Mum, Dad and Doctor Granddaughter, Brother and Sister and Doctor Granddaughter, Doctor Granddaughter with numerous friends and, tenderly and with much heartfelt affection, Doctor Granddaughter with Grandmother and Grandfather.

***

"Oh, I am just so *happy*," said Doctor Granddaughter, and she hugged the neck of her boyfriend.

"See!" said Granddad, "we're not the *only* ones here in love!"

"I can see that!" exclaimed Grandma.

Doctor Granddaughter continued gushing: "I have so many *plans!*"

Perplexed Boyfriend replied, "*We* have so many plans!"

"Yes, yes, that's what I meant! First a job…"

"Oh good!" said Dad.

"Then children and then, maybe, marriage!"

"Gosh, I'll have to return the engagement ring then!" joked Boyfriend.

Hearing this conversation followed a pattern exactly, a pattern Granddad and Grandma had sadly witnessed most of their lives: one of a gradual reversing of priorities and general disregard for the social requirements of long ago.

"Back in our day…" said Granddad.

These four words usually elicited a collective groan from anyone under eighty years old within earshot, but c'mon, not today!

"Oh now, dear, you make me sound like I'm *old!*" quipped Grandma, the life and soul of many a party for the best part of a century.

"Back in our day," he continued, "the world was in order and everything was done in order. First you courted then you kissed then you married then you had children. To have a child out of wedlock was a catastrophe."

When Grandmother heard this statement, there was a mighty thump inside her chest. This thump was not her heart but something else, something way down deep inside. The brakes had been applied to the day, somehow, and not just to the day but to something altogether more massive and costly. For a moment, the whole scene flashed as a photographic negative then returned to normal.

Finding herself looking to the left, there she saw a doorway; not a door, just the doorway, which was filled with pure black. The sunny weather did not shine into this opening even slightly. It was like a deep black cloth, door shaped, had been hung on the stone wall. The atmosphere, for her alone it seemed, changed dramatically, losing its taste and thrill to the senses and heart.

Standing now, obviously distracted and keeping focus on the black door, the usual phrases that would have accompanied such an action – "Honey, are you ok?", "Mum/Grandma…what's the matter?" – were now painfully absent. The wrench from her former life was extremely swift and brutal and yet the old woman seemed bizarrely equipped to face it as if it had been expected and prepared for all through the years on some subliminal level. It hurt to hear talk filled with joy going on behind her as she trod towards the black exit across such beautifully mown grass on a perfect sunny day. Halfway to the blackness, she turned, narrow eyed and stunned, to behold a wrenching scene.

She saw Doctor Granddaughter and yet she didn't, for now the girl's features had changed to reflect a different lineage. A new inherited strain was visible in the young woman's face. Gone was the familiar shape of the eyes, so commented on from birth. Gone also was the short stature: now, a tall and more slender person stood rejoicing on her Graduation Day. This was, again, witnessing the birth of new people who had never existed before, with personalities that had never existed before.

The old woman now glanced at "Mother", her former daughter, and, again, things had mercilessly changed. Appearance, voice, clothes: all had mercilessly changed to another family tree with different tastes. A different son-in-law sat there also, under the parasol, on this beautiful day.

She forced herself to look upon her replacement who was sitting with her back turned: a small, mocking mercy in such awfulness. Yes, this woman was old also and did indeed seem to soak up and reciprocate every drop of love, but she was the understudy, not the planned original. Had *she* lain in bed, sometimes in moonlight and sometimes not, reflecting on her beloved family? "Maybe" was as concrete an answer as would come.

Only Grandfather was unchanged. Still handsome, still attentive, still the man of true character she had fallen in love with but now knew no more, in fact never knew. Did he not see the change in his beloved wife as he pulled a small black box from his pocket?

She turned her head away sharply. The dark way was now reached. All had been erased from the past and what possible outlook was there on the other side of a dark doorway? As she stepped through, the old woman, stripped of even the remotest kind of membership of anything, heard from back at the table:

"Happy Anniversary to the prettiest girl I ever saw!"

Chapter 1: Conception

It was not the night to be out.

Those brutal beasts, whose hoof prints are told of throughout antiquity, had not forgotten their promise to return and were now demanding serfdom from all. Unopposed in every whim, spoiled with subservience of all in their path, the blizzard stallions of winter galloped and guzzled the countryside with howls and deathly swirls.

In the midst of this white anguish there was a building, strangely untouched and strangely unworried by threats of war from the north. It was quite clear this was a restaurant, hinted at by the neon sign, intermittently flashing, reluctant to be woken from its daytime slumber. One glance showed the joy of those inside.

And outside, high up on a branch festooned with talon marks, an owl sat and gazed and thought.

And inside, beautifully, most beautifully, a piano played.

***

It was not the room to be in.

Deliberately whitened hospital walls, staring with the coolest indifference, stood in rude hush, eavesdropping on the huddling young couple who sat on the hospital bed.

Outside the door, sounds of the ward: echoing footsteps, annoyingly indecipherable talk, various beeps and alarms and ringing telephones telegraphed the fact that the world was not going to stop because of mere sadness and loss. No minute silence nor even a glance over the shoulder would be given as life sped on. It was the worst kind of winter in that room: the snowless, invisible kind.

Adam sat with his arm around his tearful wife, Dolores. At a time like this, words are best kept few in number, charged with sincerity and delivered like a first kiss.

"Hey...hey, c'mon now honey."

Adam closed his eyes as sadness ravaged his expression, glad Dolores could not see this. He rubbed his hand firmly up and down Dolores' back. She buried her head into his chest and drew her legs up, partially curling into a ball of hyper fragility, sub-consciously making herself as small as possible, trying to hide from reality.

"They said it might not work, didn't they?" he continued.

Adam knew he was trying to strike a match in a hurricane. The announcement by the doctor half an hour before that the IVF treatment had failed and

Dolores had again not conceived had been cautiously foretold by said doctor in previous days, but bad news has the sharpest of edges and needs no swordsman to wield its ugly blade.

"Let's get us out of here," said Adam, gently rocking both of them back and forth. He stood up and reached awkwardly for Dolores' overnight bag, not allowing himself to break contact with her for a moment. "Let's get you home," he continued, half gasping, half sighing.

"It'll never be home now, *never*," said Dolores, throwing the crumpled, once sodden tissue she held onto the floor. Reality was hitting Dolores in waves of heat, leaving her eyes more and more drought stricken. She stood up, holding Adam's outstretched hand, and threw her arms around his neck, repeating angrily "It'll never be home now."

Adam made no reply, sensing that Dolores' angry statement was called for at that particular moment – a type of vomiting that was acceptable for a while at least. He huddle-walked his wife out the door.

***

Adam and Dolores lived in a beautiful semi-detached house – white-washed and red brick with wavy red tiles. There were just enough mature trees along the pavement and surrounding streets to help the area cross the finish line and be classed as "leafy". They had been very lucky indeed to find this gorgeous little gem at the end of a cul de sac while panning for properties three years ago.

You see, Adam and Dolores were clever people. Adam was a competent entrepreneur who helped other people get business dreams off the ground and Dolores was an interior designer who met Adam when she turned to him for said "start-up" advice. They both got on well with their parents and each other's parents and had the cliché circle of friends and "friends".

The first three or four steps to Heaven had been easy – house, cars (plural) and, well, just that secure feeling that would make living in the middle of a ploughed field seem tolerable.

All that was lacking was a child.

But this child ran like the wind, darting and dodging, as Adam and Dolores gave chase; laughing and laughing and laughing and running, staying ever ahead, and simply would not be caught and enter their lives. They had used up the three IVF attempts allowed on the NHS plus one procedure done privately. In the early days it had become something of a running joke between the couple and their parents that the child would be a long distance athlete if Dolores ever became pregnant, but jokes were now out of fashion.

A year had passed since Adam huddled his wife out of the hospital that day. It was breakfast time and the couple were chatting over coffee, cornflakes and such. Both were giggling at a story in the local paper about a lorry shedding its entire load of lemons on to someone's driveway across town.

"So, what time will you be home tonight?" asked Dolores, slipping her legs cosily around Adam's under the table. She didn't smile but the gesture spoke volumes to Adam. The "nine months after the IVF treatment" barrier had been passed. The "would have been a Mum by now" spectre, which had haunted Dolores with cruelty on four occasions, was nowadays viewed more as a seriously inconvenient fact of life – a thoughtless neighbour who played music too loud on occasion or a trip to the dentist.

But, of course, there are feelings and there are feelings. During said year, Adam had more than once glimpsed Dolores and seen those barely perceptible tell-tale signs of hidden sadness in her. Knowing her as he did, Adam knew his wife carried sore pangs of unfulfilled longing.

The year had passed quickly because, if time is the great healer, then keeping busy is a hungry dog, devouring days and weeks, even hours and minutes. As long as it serves you, this ravenous canine will gobble anything you throw its way, refusing only the detestable taste of idleness. Adam and Dolores had indeed kept busy, the coping mechanism had worked and now fifty-two weeks had flown by.

"Just the normal time. Fancy going to the cinema or something?" replied Adam with a smile. His smile leapt across the table and infected Dolores' countenance. She beamed back at him with wide eyes.

"Yes! Good idea! Can I choose?"

Adam sensed an impending "chick-flick", but any port in a storm.

"Yeah, great!" It was a "*he knew* that *she knew* that *he knew*" moment. They both laughed.

***

Working day over, Adam walked back out to his car. It had been a sunny day with just the odd paper-thin cloud dabbed onto the blue. He opened the car door and stood staring at what promised to be a beautiful summer evening. Adam always parked under one of the few trees that were in the car park to ensure at least partial shade on a day just like today. He put his briefcase in the back seat then jumped into the front. Taking shade into account, the interior was still nearly roasting and Adam turned on the ignition then lowered all four windows.

He had just put on his seatbelt when something bounced off the bonnet of the car onto the ground. Knowing instantly that it was something more than a twig, more like a little white acorn, Adam undid the seatbelt and got out to look. There, level with the front of the car, was a bird's egg.

"Oh no! Oh no!" said Adam, now with a worried countenance. He hurriedly bent and gently picked up the fallen egg in hope but it felt cold. Adam held the little capsule of potential life and just stared at it. The egg was brown speckled on sky blue and fairly tiny. The brown speckles looked like they had been applied with the most casual flick of a finger dipped in dark paint, almost accidental, in fact. The combination of colours and pattern, as childishly simple as it was, demanded consideration and were hypnotic unto Adam, who just stared and stared at it. Really? Could this be? Can such a thing happen – one man's entire world slammed to a halt by a tiny bird's egg?

Turning the egg slightly, Adam saw a hole where the chick had begun to peck through to life. The hole was filled with congealed blood, signifying that the battle for emerging life was sadly lost. This jolted Adam somewhat. Surely beauty must live forever, surely. The two lines of thought clashed horribly. As Adam held this symbol of unfulfilled potential, he realised that the egg had never existed before in all history and would never come again. Who knew how this feathered story would have unfolded? He stroked the egg tenderly and then found himself pressing it carefully against his heart.

There was a waste bin just the other side of the car and Adam placed the egg on top then took some drive-thru napkins out of the glove compartment and wrapped the egg in several of them. There were some bushes nearby. Adam knelt and scooped a hole in the ground underneath them, placed the egg within then gently covered it with earth and patted it down, swithering as to whether to tell Dolores or not as Dolores also took such things deeply to heart.

"We met just a little too late, buddy, but that does not stop me calling you 'friend'," said Adam, returning to his car.

It suddenly hit him that today, this exact calendar date, like the egg, had never been before in all history and would never come again. It had finally arrived only to be taken for granted and all but ignored by the entire human race, slumping off dejectedly into historical oblivion to be pined for, many years from now, by the regretfully nostalgic. Both the poor unborn sparrow and the day on which it died were utterly ignored and wasted by just about everybody. But Adam *had* stopped and stood and gazed and thought. He *had* noticed them, both of them. He had acknowledged that which, by default, is readily ignored.

As he drove out of the car park, he smilingly braced himself for the forthcoming rom com. "*What is it with women?*" he thought. Men need a twelve-hour warning for such cinematic experiences but Dolores could compete at international level on these films. It was Dolores' love for the genre that helped put a rich vein of light-heartedness into the marriage, which is maybe what attracted Adam to her to begin with.

Adam drove and stopped and drove and stopped in rush hour traffic as workers from all parts of the city eagerly turned escapologist and exited as if fleeing some natural disaster. He looked around at them and wondered what they were wondering. The faces of these people were hard to read but not a smile could be seen – that much *was* legible. Either these people had nothing to go home to or too much to go home to, because, as being bullied did not end when you took off your school uniform for the last time, weighty concerns did not start at nine and finish at five.

Eventually, "drove" began to outnumber "stopped" and "no city" began to outnumber "city". Normally, Adam smiled at this point but this time his smile was curtailed somewhat as he realised that "enduring a rom com" was now outnumbering "feet up – watching highlights of the football".

Chapter 2: First Contraction

Suddenly, night fell in one blink and, *snap,* daylight was gone!

Extremely forceful, bullying snow and wind surrounded Adam's car, inflicting fright and shock on him. Disrespectfully and with no time for dawning realisation, a cacophony of ancient frozen hooves, stabled in the bosom of anger, meticulously weaned on downtrodden and crushed man, arrived in shuddering command.

"*Woah!*" Adam shouted as he slammed on the brakes, making the car skid a semi-pirouette in snow already inches deep mere seconds after arrival. Remembering that two cars had just been a short distance behind and that he was now in the wrong lane facing the wrong way, Adam sprang from the car, arms waving desperately and screaming a very loud and elongated "*Stop!*" But there were no following cars and no promised summer's evening.

Sheer panic was now eaten in one gulp by mystification in this flash bang of hurtling whiteness in pitch darkness, the presence of which had now evicted the real world with kingly ease. Mature trees did their stubborn, creaking best to rebel against the wrenching gale and simply refused to back down, bending in defiance, not homage. Adam's mind and racing heart juggled adrenaline, fright and stun between them with scary dexterity. He had seen his route home in all seasons, repeatedly, but *did not recognise this road*.

With bizarre reciprocation, the road did not recognise *him*. Status, it would seem, was a social currency not accepted in this suddenly land. Adam spun around, having sprinted 100 yards or so to warn the gone cars and – amidst the whirl and swirl – saw his car with hazards flashing, lighting up the perfect circle his pirouette skid had made. He jogged back to the car, more falling than sitting into the seat, door open, one leg out, snow splattered and gasping and wondering and staring and unprepared and caught off guard. The starting gun had sounded and now thoughts raced: *"Wait…stop…police, no…call Dolores…sit it out…get out of here…just…just"*

But there it was: Adam was in this tumult, on his own in this tumult, miles from sweet Dolores in this tumult. Putting on his seatbelt, Adam allowed the car to move slowly forward, back the way he came, virgin snow creaking underneath.

***

The back and forth of wipers saved Adam from being hypnotised by the beauty of thick snowflakes tearing past, allowing him to concentrate, moving slowly around never encountered before bends and along unfamiliar straights. *He would call Dolores the moment he could safely pull over*. Why had no one either at work or on TV even *mentioned* this?

But then, a way off, a flash of red. Adam slammed the brakes, still a fair skid even at slow speed. *Someone else had been ambushed* it appeared. Adam felt a connection with this poor traveller immediately. The red light flashed on and off intermittently, showing drive a few yards then brake then repeat and repeat. The passing snow and the wipers continued with their duel. *I'll just follow this guy back to town then call Dolores*. Suddenly, more lights came into view, dull ambers and blues, not blinding, more welcoming than warning. The red light, still flashing, was in the midst of this. "Oh no, an accident!" muttered Adam.

It was safe to approach at this speed so Adam drove, as close as he dared, intending to offer assistance. But all thoughts of his road companion and the connection Adam felt with him now vanished as it became suddenly clear this was a restaurant, not a pile up; the dabbing brake lights of the fellow traveller were in fact the restaurant's neon sign.

"What...I mean just *what?*"

Partially shielded from the blizzard by this suddenly building, Adam opened his car door and once again sat one leg out, unprepared and caught off guard. This was indeed a surprise and was indeed a restaurant! There was much movement inside and warmth inside and a beckoning like Adam had never felt before. He could hear a piano playing. Caught between being stunned and delighted, Adam did neither and called Dolores.

"Hi, yeah…no, it's ok nothing's wrong…I've been caught in a blizzard…I know…yeah a real blizzard with real snow…look, if I was having an affair I would have a better excuse than *this!*…this restaurant has come to my rescue…it's called…" He looked at the neon sign properly for the first time, it said:

TED

"'Ted'…it…it's called 'Ted's'…no, I've never heard of it either…I'll sit this out here. Ok…look, I'm sorry, but it's out of my hands…call you in a while… Ok, I'll tell her I'm already spoken for!"

Getting out to make a dash inside, Adam paused and saw that he was in a car park with bays for at least 100 cars. *I would have known about this place opening, or Dolores would have.* Ten seconds later and Adam pushed the door open. *Oh, the relief!*

Chapter 3: Second Contraction

Yes, oh, the relief and, oh, the warmth and, *oh*, such kindly cacophony of pleasant dining chatter woven in with the playing piano. The air was thick with mouth-watering smells and fulfilment. No sooner in the door but Adam was jostled from behind by smiling and excited arriving diners: a young woman holding the hand of a little girl, a man in his fifties closely followed by two elderly people whom Adam assumed to be a couple. They were all dressed inappropriately for such weather, obviously caught out as he had been. *But they had not been in the car park or I would have seen them. Where are their vehicles?* thought Adam, looking out the window to see only his car outside, inches-deep snow upon the windscreen.

Adam's unexpected entourage all greeted him with a pleasant "Good evening!" then giggled their way off into the depths of what Adam now saw was an unusually big restaurant. Size, however, did not diminish quaintness and already Adam intended he and Dolores to be regulars.

In this mixture of confusion and delighted discovery, Adam stopped a passing waitress:

"Excuse me miss, can I get a table please?"

"*Get a table?*" She looked and sounded as if Adam

had just asked her to solve a Rubik's Cube with the lights off.

"Yes, and where do I hang my coat?"

"*Hang my coat!* Do you *mean* that?"

Adam's perplexed look was answer enough to this abrupt and bizarre question. The waitress hurried to the window and looked out at Adam's car, putting her hand over her gaping mouth. Adam felt guilty of violating some in-house, unwritten rule.

"Look, I know this is sudden but the snow…"

The waitress, still with her hand over her mouth, felt Adam's coat arm, squeezing the wet fabric; an invasion of personal space. She lowered her hand very slowly, mouth still agape, all the while beholding Adam with eyes unready, either sparkling or welling up. A look of startled mingled with craving.

"I'll get the manager." She briskly walked away, nearly stumbling, looking back over her shoulder at Adam, leaving him stranded and confused, much as he had been outside. He so didn't want his first visit here to be tainted with offence.

While waiting with jostling emotions, Adam gazed around and it was at this point that certain oddities became apparent. Seemingly, there was an unusual formula governing how people arrived and where they sat. Firstly, everybody who arrived, whether grouped or single, was inappropriately dressed for the weather and just "arrived", with no vehicles coming or going or parked outside. Little children, completely on their own, would occasionally come running through the door excitedly, and, like all other arriving diners, be inappropriately dressed for a snowstorm and with no accompanying adults at all, yet no one showed the slightest concern.

The other part of this formula concerned seating. It was clear some sort of strange yet welcome segregation was afoot. You see, in any given restaurant the usual thing is for people to sit in the expected groups – a family of four; a candle-lit couple at the start of a relationship or a solitary figure at the end of one; a hen party or stag do, over-noisy and over-animated; and the usual lone businessman at a corner table, in straining pretence that his mobile phone is the only company he needs.

But things were different here.

Entering groups would immediately split up and go in different directions. The elderly would move slowly but with happy purpose to sit with other elderly, and not just a few but tables and tables of them, laughing at what Adam assumed were a lifetime of anecdotes. The middle aged would enter and go to any number of tables exclusively set aside for their age group where there was no mention of middle age spread, cellulite, unfulfilling careers and hair loss, just beaming merriment. Young adults and children followed suit and sat with their own, cheerily chatting the language of their age.

But what was oddest of all was that little children sat at tables given completely over to them, with apparently no adults paying any parental, or at least token parental, attention. Their tables were indeed scenes of childhood confusion with teetering drinks and babble yet no one complained or corrected the naturally boisterous and they were left to their antics. Adults who walked by simply laughed at the merriment then walked on.

Adam's eyes scanned back and forth at this odd set up. His face had not stopped showing confusion almost since arrival and little wonder really. Suddenly, from behind: "Good evening, Sir!"

One look told Adam this was the manager – the same height as Adam but ten years older and very professional, almost slick, in his ability to make a diner feel special. But even someone who can shuffle an entire pack of cards with one hand, and has done so for years, will occasionally drop a few and this manager could not totally hide the fact that, to *him*, Adam was an outstanding curiosity and was staggered to see him.

"Teri-An tells me you've escaped…er…reality and have sought refuge with us!"

Adam looked over the manager's shoulder at Teri-An, who was standing in attendance. Her face already bore a sincere smile but eye to eye contact can polish a smile to perfection and now she beamed even more.

"Well, yes, yes I have!" replied Adam. "It really took me by surprise, I mean the storm and this place and you folks and everything!"

At this point, the smile on the manager's face was thrust aside by an expression worryingly ambiguous.

He repeated what Adam had just said, word for word, but semi-muttering, slowly and deliberately – all the while holding Adam's gaze with the squinting eyes of a man marvelling. Teri-An also squinted. She was marvelling also, but through her smile, not in place of it. Seeing this brought relief to Adam, who was beginning to have thoughts of braving the storm again. For a few heavy moments akin to watching a spinning coin slide and spin and slow and slow to its rattling decision, Adam could only wait. He thought of Dolores.

The manager turned to Teri-An. They both nodded in agreement; they both smiled.

"Teri-An, please see this gentleman to his table." He turned to face Adam. "And show him a menu!" Teri-An bowed slightly toward Adam and extended her arm towards a table. "Sir, please, this way!"

Adam now knew, once and for all, the meaning of the word "relief", the feeling of which came with a whoosh. Teri-An led on, so happy to be dealing with Adam that her smile was almost visible on the back of her head.

The relief and happiness Adam felt, spiced with the taste of what, for him, was a flickering reminder of boyhood adventures, drew his attention away from something – for now, every single diner, even jostling children, ceased conversing and stared at Adam. Only the piano spoke on, kindly veiling this potentially unnerving behaviour from Adam's view as he took his seat.

***

Gradually returning chatter accompanied Adam's seating at the table, and what a table! Solid oak, with determined streaks of bronzed grain that preached the Gospel of Asymmetry, edged in woven marquetry that was a breathtaking Celtic-style chase of swirls and dips and rises. In amongst the giggling race of the marquetry there were words written. Adam, just so overwhelmed by it all, saw the words but didn't really read them.

The table was decked in such finery with shouting silver where it was created for and soft comforting fabric where it was created for and everything oh so personal! *"All this for just me?"* is not normally something asked by a diner even in the best places as quality is expected, but Adam asked himself exactly that as it was all so unusually beautiful. Suddenly, a joyous Teri-An intruded on his thoughts:

"Well, Sir, heerree is your *MENU!*" she said jovially, plonking a pretty menu right into Adam's hands. Adam thought Dolores and Teri-An would get along famously – he *knew* they would! He surmised that Teri-An, like Dolores, had a wide circle of cheery friends and that they would adopt each other into the other's sisterhood immediately. Adam was so happy now! A look at the cover of the menu drew a smile as Adam muttered the words he saw:

"Be happy, today may be your birthday!"

"I like that!" chuckled Adam. "And when's your birthday, Teri-An?"

"Oh, I don't have a birthday!" she replied, holding up a defensive hand, shaking her head in denial, smiling.

"Yeah, that's what my wife says! I can see us both being regulars here at Ted's!"

"Ted's?" replied Teri-An, with a puzzled look.

"Yes, this place *is* called Ted's, isn't it?"

"No, it's…oh, I see what's happened. I'll get the sign fixed again!"

"But it's working just fine, it…"

"I'll give you a few minutes!" she said, and attended a nearby table.

So Adam perused the menu much as he had perused the lovely oddities of the restaurant and the diners had perused *him*. Knowing that years from now he would look back to this moment with craving, Adam just sat and tried to taste the moment with his feelings – to look around and taste with sight; to close the eyes and taste with sound; to pave an easy and idyllic path for his thoughts to return to this particular evening one day. Adam stared at the wording on the menu's cover as he ran his fingers over the beautifully embossed lettering on sweet red velvet – his favourite colour, no less! He wanted time to stand still.

Suddenly, Adam became aware of a very elderly lady standing next to him, staring at him intently. She reached out and took his hand. For a moment Adam thought maybe he was in her pre-booked seat and was just about to excuse himself and move or offer any gentlemanly assistance he could when she spoke:

"How odd we should see each other like this
– and now a kiss!"

Adam smiled…"Sorry, have we met before?"

She leaned in towards Adam who, momentarily anaesthetised by her strange words, instinctively leaned towards her. The kiss from the old lady arrived on Adam's cheek in a burst of bliss. Adam drew sharp breath as he felt memories of things he had never experienced being implanted into his own. It was a 'wow' moment. The pretty menu fell to the table as he drew breath very sharply and very nearly wept. The lady stroked Adam's cheek a single time with wonderful tenderness then walked on, leaving Adam staring over his shoulder at her. When he looked back around, Adam saw nearly every other diner smiling at him. It was obvious they knew something he didn't.

Picking up the pretty menu again, Adam gave another look over his shoulder but the old woman was gone. Adam now knew he was somewhere not normal, somewhere strange yet so very friendly and longing to become acquainted like he was shaking hands with a smiling giant and didn't know if he should flee or let be. Adam didn't know whether it showed on his face and by now he didn't really care.

***

It did not surprise Adam that the menu was equally as pretty once opened and, added to that, he felt something in the air was prohibiting him from taking the beauty for granted. Everything seen, heard and felt since his arrival was, it seemed, prolonged unto him. Teri-An cheerfully gate crashed the moment.

"The soup is always nice!" she gushed.

"What…? Oh…yes…yes, go on then, Teri-An!"

As Teri-An smiled and walked off, Adam heard someone knocking on a door. He looked around and saw the snowstorm still at full strength, then "*Knock*" – there it was again! It took a few more knocks till Adam located the door. He thought of the person caught out as he had been and started to rise to let the poor soul in as nobody else, unsurprisingly by now, seemed to bother. But, before he could even stand up, several of the children, a young man and a more mature-looking woman went to the door and opened it.

"*Well, good on you!*" thought Adam.

The door opened and *light* gushed in! No snow flurry, no thankful, windswept traveller, just light that almost sang with purity. The small entourage, who had opened the door, momentarily cast shadows then rushed with all eagerness into the brightness and were gone, taking their shadows with them. The door did not close but remained open – the light shone on. People walked past and dining chatter continued. Was Adam the only one aware of what had just happened? He certainly thought so. Teri-An arrived with the promised soup.

"Did you see that?" asked Adam.

"Yes, I did!"

"Well, what *was* it? Who was knocking?"

Teri-An replied, "He who stands at the door and knocks is..." she went wide eyed and playfully shrugged her shoulders, "...he who stands at the door and...well...*knocks!!!*"

"But why did those particular people go through?"

"Because they were fully satisfied!"

"With what? The meal?"

Teri-An laughed. "*NO!* They were satisfied with all the wonderful experiences life had to offer and wanted to move on!"

"Move on? Where to? But some were just children? How could they possibly...?"

Teri-An touched Adam's shoulder lovingly.

"Your soup is getting cold!"

Adam looked down at the delightful broth as the aroma rose and pleased him greatly. He picked up the spoon and looked over to the door, which had now closed. Finally, at last and not a moment too soon, Adam began to enjoy his meal! Oh, the taste of such savoury satisfaction: full bodied, fulfilling, and, perfectly, just one step short of too hot to enjoy! Such a sensory thaw! With crustless bread to hand and curvaceous silver *in* his hand, Adam dined more and smiled more. Dolores would enjoy hearing of all this again and again!

It was when, lifting the second or third last spoonful to his mouth, that Adam noticed wording round the edge of the bowl. He paused, spoon in mid air, and, with concentrating countenance, read:

A spider is ugly and ugly he roams
Not wanted outside nor in peoples' homes!

A statuesque Adam read and re-read this bizarre and unkind little saying and forgot about those last two or three mouthfuls. The soup had been so delicious, yet, all the while, had been betrothed to these awful and puzzling words. There was an underlying vein of *something* about this whole place.

Still with squinting concentration, Adam looked and saw Teri-An in joyous conversation with other diners. She kept an eye on Adam, continually glancing his way, not with waiting staff attention but with something far deeper and more serious. Adam noticed this and for the first time became aware that an invisible thirst was being quenched. With each and every interaction since entering, Adam had been experiencing a subtle watering – a subtle hydration he felt was bringing him to a life-point he would otherwise miss.

"And how was the soup, Sir?" Adam looked up to see the manager.

"Delicious, well and truly! "

"Well I'm 'well and truly' pleased!" the manager replied.

Adam took the opportunity to ask: "Excuse me, but a few minutes ago an elderly lady came up to me and it was the oddest encounter!"

"I'm sure it was, Sir, but nice at the same time, dare I say?"

"Well…yes, but I just wondered…"

"Teri-An knows the lady well, don't you Teri-An?"

Teri-An was suddenly right there holding a plate laden with deliciousness. She daintily and caringly lowered it in front of Adam and seasoned it with her lovely smile.

"Yes! She and I appear to be on the same wavelength!"

"Well…I never really thought…"

Adam stopped mid sentence as he realised Teri-An had brought him his all-time favourite meal – without Adam giving his order. A succulence of salmon, courted and wooed by surrounding baby potatoes and vegetables, all under a comfort of lemon butter sauce, delighted the sight and flooded Adam's watering mouth. Like the soup dish, there were words around the edge of the plate and this time Adam read them immediately:

Sleek Fox is so handsome and handsome he roams
But he is also not wanted outside nor in homes!

Teri-An stood by and knew Adam was now crossing a threshold.

Her smile was now gone only to be replaced with the look of almost parental care. Adam looked up at her, reached forth, and took her hand. Longing trumped protocol and yearning conquered etiquette.

"Teri-An, where am I?"

She sat down opposite Adam, still holding his hand, and replied...

Chapter 4: Third Contraction

"You are where years, and there may be many of those years, are restored to their rightful owners. You are where unfortunates become flush with a wealth of time, for the Architect who made this place designed it for us. Our world is similar to yours but in your world a most terrible thing exists called loss. Here there is only gain and the truest satisfaction. We can stay here as long as we like before we move on."

"That bright door that opened?"

"Yes. Those people had reached a point where they were more than satisfied with their life experiences. You noticed that some were just children and wondered how can a mere child be satisfied with all life has to offer? That is because when people come here they come at the age they would have enjoyed the most had they lived in your world; a very clever design twist by the Architect."

Just then, a beautiful little boy ran past, laughing to burst. Teri-An called to him: "C'mere a second, Samuel honey!" Samuel turned and jumped on Teri-An's knee. The two embraced, displaying a bond that would make any two, anywhere, jealous.

"OW, you are a rascal! How old are you, Samuel?" asked Teri-An as she fought to control Mr Giggly on her knee.

"Twelve!"

"What! You are *never* twelve!"

"Twenty-three!"

"You're twelve *and* twenty-three! Oh wow, how d'ya manage *that?!*" said Teri-An, pretending to be impressed but certainly not pretending to love.

Samuel jumped down and ran off, laughing to burst. He turned and waved and Teri-An reciprocated. She continued to talk to Adam while still looking lovingly at Samuel: "Here, children differ slightly from us adults in that there is more than one way they can arrive. Those you saw go through the door had soaked up and enjoyed those restored years and chose to move through the Way."

"You say 'the Way' as if it's the only one."

"It is. Do you see the door you came through?"

Adam turned and looked to see dribs and drabs of people arriving as they had when he himself arrived. He turned to look at Teri-An again.

"Do you see anybody *leaving* through that door?" she asked. Adam's expression was answer enough.

"Eat up, it's your favourite!" said Teri-An, alighting from her seat. She squeezed Adam's shoulder, continuing: "And *don't worry*, you're among friends!"

The salmon was simply exquisite but Adam ate pensively. The meal was truly delicious but he felt small and humbled. He was now fully aware that two threads – the immensely serious and the immensely loving – ran, hand in hand, throughout the setting. The wafting and lilting piano playing wandered throughout all this like some benevolent Harlequin, unseen but pouring blessed water on to hidden and unspoken thirsts. Oh, poor Harlequin, doing so much yet unseen and unappreciated. Such a silent and lonesome occupation. So *how* exactly does one become a Harlequin? One clue is to be acrobatic minus some degree(s) of speech. But Harlequins aside, Adam knew he was someplace rare and had been invited by someone gracious, someone beautiful.

***

Still half here and half in deep thought, Adam finished his glass of wine and twirled the glass slowly, watching as the light flirted with the cut crystal. Suddenly,

"This is for you, Sir!"

Adam looked to see a beautiful girl aged about eight standing holding a dessert.

"Well, what's *your* name?" asked Adam with a broad smile.

"I am the Child of Three Keys, the offspring of rejection and longing," was the beautiful girl's smiling, immediate and mystifying answer. As she said this she placed the bowl of sweet and colourful delights in front of Adam as Teri-An removed the main course plate from the other side. Just the smell of the sophisticated sweetness made Adam's eyes close in reflex and frown with savage delight. Adam eventually opened his eyes, looked down, and read the words around the bowl's edge:

"Soft Babe, why are you here?"
Fox and Spider ask Child.
*"We know **we** are outcasts, but **you** are not wild!"*

Adam, at the reading of this, was now only capable of sitting in silence. He had been dealt a double blow, firstly by the beautiful little girl delivering words of such magnitude with such a pretty smile on her face and secondly by the wording on the bowl, which spoke of social expulsion, which spoke of thorny, barbed and stinging exclusion, perhaps the ugliest emotion a person can experience. The words Adam had heard and read since entering – and the very place he had entered – demanded reconciliation. He felt he would either leave with the answers or simply die.

But then, remembering the charming young lady standing next to him, Adam smiled broadly for her again. "Well, all this yummy delight seems too much for one person! Why don't we get you a spoon and we can take on the challenge together!"

The dainty maiden reached out and took the spoon from Adam's hand, apparently accepting his hopeful invitation. Oh, how glad Adam was! Such a dining companion would thrill the heart of a statue! Adam saw Teri-An nearby and was just about to request a spoon for himself when the girl replaced the spoon on the table next to the bowl. Adam looked at her and, through a smile which now had to be more forced, felt doubt that threatened to become disappointment. But the girl smiled a sophisticated balm of a smile, curtsied and held out a beckoning hand to Adam.

"May I have this dance?" she said, in a tone that would make an angel jealous.

Oh, the depth of gasping, smiling surprise that rose in Adam's heart at hearing this fragile invitation! An invitation loaded with adventure! An invitation that promised to keep its promises! An utter oath of an invitation! An invitation and an invocation! Adam looked towards Teri-An, who nodded her head with a "Go ahead!" smile. The little girl took Adam's hand and led on. Adam's heart rose to its feet; his body merely followed.

Chapter 5: Birth

The piano playing was suddenly conspicuous by its absence. The dining chatter ceased and the Harlequin slept. Everything – Teri-An, every single diner, tables, chairs – *everything* was gone! Only two pairs of footsteps could be heard, walking on the wooden floor. Adam glanced around to see all was gone. A dusk of emotion had descended, bringing physical darkness with it. But the girl, however, knew her way. The darkness could not engulf her and Adam saw her clearly, suddenly feeling ever so proud just to be acknowledged and befriended by her. Oh, the "Why?" of it all.

After walking a while, the girl slowed her step and turned to face her friend. They both came to a stop, facing each other. The girl let go of Adam's hand and threw her arms around his waist, squeezing him tightly as she pressed her cheek into his stomach. Adam drew a sharp breath and started crying. The girl, hearing this, said "Yes, cry my friend, cry, for tears can never lie!" Adam wrapped his arms around the child of rejection and longing and both stood in light and warmth, rooted and grounded in love right to the core of the world.

The girl looked up into Adam's dripping, red eyes.

"Now, how about our dance?"

"Yes, how about it?" stuttered Adam.

The girl placed her feet on top of Adam's, the way children do.

"You show me how to dance and I will show you what I know!" she said.

Adam was just about to say, "I'd love that!", when he realised that he and the girl were now surrounded by other little children roughly the same age as his young friend, and not just a few but a breathtaking hoard of them – breathtaking to the point of being frightening. Dozens and dozens, massing till it became hundreds of children, completely out of nowhere, gathered to watch the dance. Adam looked around but the girl just looked at him and laughed at his surprise. The children sat in a large circle, with each row higher than the one in front. The sight was simply spectacular. Adam would have stared at all this for much longer but the girl took Adam's right hand in her left, placed Adam's arm around her waist, and put her hand on his shoulder. Adam was now defenceless in her hands and at her mercy.

And the daughter of rejection and longing said "*Go!*"

With this, the piano resumed. Harlequins awoke and rubbed sand from their eyes. Adam, the girl and the piano joined forces and began to weave an atmosphere as a loom loaded with threads of the purest and refined friendliness. The girl looked down at her feet upon Adam's then into Adam's eyes as Adam looked down at his feet under the girl's and into *hers!* Soon, neither could stop laughing! Dancing a fun waltz – so normal and fun, just so "real-worldly" and fun! On and on went the plodding pair! Now and then the girl would let go of Adam's hands and just squeeze him round his waist with a giggle! Every child spectator applauded and laughed!

In the midst of this righteous revelry, the girl let go of Adam's waist and put her left hand on his temple with something of a slap and pressed her right hand with equal vigour on his heart. Suddenly an outpouring of experience and an up-flowing of awesomeness – from the girl into Adam – began. Dancing, whatever kind of waltz it was, now ceased, as Adam became so overwhelmed he just sobbingly sank to his knees, both hands covering his eyes either from shame or embarrassment.

Once on his knees, the girl broke her grip and cuddled Adam's head into her neck with a tenderness not known in Adam's world. Now a touch was as a voice unto Adam, and, through her cradling touch alone, the child sang the lullaby to the man – soft, warm and extremely comforting in the near darkness. Everything was just so saturated with care and concern.

Again, very softly this time, the girl placed a hand on Adam's temple and very gently slid her other hand under Adam's arms, which were still covering his eyes, and onto his heart. Now that the child saw Adam was calmed somewhat, the impartation could continue.

Down in his heart or up in his head, Adam knew not exactly where, but with his eyes tightly closed, and those eyes tightly guarded by his arms, he saw things.

Curled hands he saw, mighty and strong. At once these hands unfurled, and out fell worlds innumerable. Now these worlds tumbled, rolled and fell, and, as they unfurled out of their confusion, out fell the Earth. Near the break of day it was on the Earth, and, as Adam knelt in the girl's unusually warm grip, he saw the daylight unfurl and out fell such a mosaic of green. Oh, it was a green of beginnings, a green to tell of, the green of the Fields of Life! To see these fields from afar was to rejoice but to walk upon them was to live forever! Blessed green unfurled and out fell a young couple, running hand in hand towards a beautiful grassy crest. Everything was just so *new!*

Unfurling hands, mighty and strong, frightening to see but benevolent in intent, released a second time. Now an avalanche of scrolls made from creaky parchment tumbled forth down upon the Earth. Down fell myriads of scrolls, tied with pink or blue ribbons that rippled through the air like the mane of Pegasus. On and on and on fell this rain of written life! Now the running couple, laughingly caught out in this downpour of calligraphic excellence and only just visible amidst the scrolls, reached the crest. Every scroll that landed bounced with a pleasantly pleasing "plink" sound then rolled to rest.

Back at the dance, Adam lowered his arms slightly and opened his eyes to meet the most loving expression he had ever seen on his young friend's face. Under his arm, the girl curled her fingers slightly, digging into Adam's breast. Till now, it had been her fingertips that were touching Adam's right temple but now she pressed her whole hand against him. Telling these motions were and Adam knew there was more to see. He knew that she knew he had opened his eyes. Adam knew she wanted him to follow suit and closed his eyes again to see the young couple reach out and grab a falling scroll. Tied with a pink ribbon was this curled up and as yet un-read life story. Immediately, the young man knelt before his love as if proposing marriage. Gratefully, the woman looked down upon the man's gesture as he pressed the scroll against her stomach. Now both pressed and the scroll vanished into the woman with joy!

On went the lullaby embrace of the girl!

The moment the scroll was absorbed into the woman's belly, down in the glade before them, appeared a children's playground. Terrific fun was being had by about a dozen or so children on those swings, slides, seesaws and roundabouts. Happy wasn't the word for it really as these children were in their element, enjoying those playthings and, without realising it, each other.

Enjoying himself back at the dance and in his friend's embrace – was Adam!

Now he saw that the playground was surrounded by a fence and that his young friend stood outside with longing. Doubtless there was an entrance though and she would gain entry. On went the relentless carnival within. Finding no gate, the girl ran round the side then the back and round the other side, back to where she first stood, but no gate was found by Adam's hopeful friend. You would really have to witness this sad sight as Adam did to appreciate the heart-wrenching disappointment of his young sweetheart. Ostracised without even knowing of the word's existence.

Up close, Adam saw the fence now and saw that it was made of barbed wire and savage thorns. "*Really?*" thought a now truly indignant Adam, "*You would go to such ugly lengths to keep the little girl out?*" Sadness flooded Adam's heart now, a mere sample of what his young friend was feeling. Terrible was the sight and terrible was Adam's inability to right the wrong. Once a child himself, Adam wanted to look away, to lift his friend from her nasty fate, but could do neither. Realising entry would never be hers, her young and ponytailed head sank, yet the vision persisted, despite Adam wanting to pick up the girl and just run away, run anywhere, to happier surroundings.

Mother and Father now reached their girl. At once they saw her misery and knelt either side of her. Kisses rained down from them both as all three huddled, a crumb of comfort at least. Eventually, Father stood and walked to the hurtful boundary fence. Now he reached forth and snapped off three thorns. "*Odd behaviour!*" thought Adam.

Delaying for a second to view the playing children within, he returned, thorns in hand and knelt with his family. Expectantly and automatically, mother and daughter both held out a hand and a thorn was placed in each. Lovely hands that belonged in dusty old paintings now held potential pain and actual ugliness. All three now closed their hands tightly around those thorns. Yes, the fragile and perfect took pain upon themselves. A cry like Adam had never heard went up from the beautiful child as the ugly stabbed into her palm. Crying that went up and up to darken anything it met shocked Adam so much he would have fallen backwards onto the floor had the girl, who seemed to be made from iron at this point, not held him.

Callously, blood flowed out through her clenched fist, but the grip was not relaxed. Each parent held their fists over hers and let blood flow down on to her already bloodied hand. Putting their arms around their daughter, the three stood united in the joy of love and the pain of true sacrifice. Tempting as it was to release and be relieved, the three held on and on as others laughed and played just yards away.

Just when it seemed all three would die, the tears being shed by the girl fell heavily, washing away blood from her young hand. Every drop of sadness claimed a drop of blood as its prey. Soon the hand, although still tightly clenched, was washed as clean as that of a newborn. Unswerving in her task, crying over but eyes so red from the many tears shed, the girl now opened her little hand – her parents looked and smiled – Adam looked with utter astonishment. Sitting on her hand was a key – a strange-looking key.

The three stood anew now, it seemed. On first glance, a person would not notice any difference, but Adam, still locked into this vision back in her arms, saw new posture, new expressions and new future.

Do you ever really think about it? All over the world and all the time, keys are unlocking something. You approach the door or gate or whatever and all you can think of is what lies on the other side. Today, your family may be the other side of that door and, tomorrow, your place of work. Having the correct key is more than just a case of gaining access though, isn't it? Every key has a status and if you own the correct key of the correct status then you are truly honoured. Now, the key to your office may be important to you, but what lies behind that door apart from filing cabinets, computers and endless, bland paperwork? Much responsibility – but little honour – lies with that particular key.

Every key was made by someone. Every key was forged somewhere. Times past saw the heat of the forge melting and the silversmith sweating but, today, keys are made in minutes at the push of a button. Maybe you have never thought that other keys exist – well, they do, don't they? Every time you meet a stranger is not your smile a key you turn, hoping to unlock a friendship? And did it work? Not every key fits every lock as you will have found out by now, causing you sadness. Did the potential friend fail to realise just what you offered? Location of these keys, these invisible but vastly superior keys, is where exactly? Of what cost are they and can they in fact be bought? Verily, verily, they are forged in the heart, are they not? Each year passing in time is the melting pot and life's experiences are the silversmith, do you not think?

Much to his horror, Adam saw that the key the girl held had taken rejection and longing to design and undeserved pain to fashion and hammer into shape. Even an innocent heart plunged into volcanic heat was required, for only the searing can melt this particular raw material and sweet and simple hands alone are trusted not to drop the unbearable till fashion is spent. Indeed, the Architect uses what others call weak to achieve his feats of strength.

Now the girl reached into her heart and pulled out the scroll. Glorious pink silk held the parchment closed. Leaning in as close as the vision would allow, Adam felt cheated to the point of agony as he craved above all to see the words written. Oh, what taunting was this? Really? Yearnings squatted in Adam's heart as the girl took the strange-looking key and the scroll, ran over a crest out of sight and...

ENOUGH! Adam was back in the girl's arms! The vision was over, the amphitheatre of children was gone, but the meeting was certainly not. Adam's dance partner released her embrace and stood eye to eye with him as Adam was still on his knees. He opened his eyes. The pair smiled and laughed, she easily, Adam not so easily, considering what he had just witnessed.

"I have something for you!" said the girl.

"I think you've given me more than my share," replied Adam, head bowed in humility.

She held up her right hand and there, in her palm, was the strange-looking key. What made this key strange was that it was three keys joined at one end. Adam could immediately see that the keys were all cut differently but because they were so joined they could never open any ordinary lock.

The girl simply looked, not stared, into Adam's eyes, her smile slipping and slipping and slipping until her eyes took over and spoke to Adam:

"To you I offer the Key of Three Keys my friend, for it was not made for me but for thee! "

Adam reached out and the strange Key of Three Keys was placed in his hand. It felt extremely warm from the girl's touch. He stared at the key, transfixed by its other-worldly craftsmanship. Much responsibility – and honour unspeakable – lay with this key most fantastic that lay warmly in Adam's hand and was now – at excruciating price – his. Obtained through great strain yet given away with ease. His friend waited patiently. When Adam looked up, the girl rolled her eyes upwards and nodded her head upwards to invite Adam to look up at something. Adam took his cue, looked up and, *WHOOSH*, the girl blew a short sharp breath up into Adam's nostrils.

And the first person went to live in Adam's heart.

He looked down at his friend with that look you give your child when they've successfully played a trick on you.

"Look at the key now!" said the girl.

Adam looked and one of the keys had now disappeared, leaving two, still joined. Adam closed his eyes, smiled and nodded in acceptance. What world is this, where the miraculous is the norm? Once again, the girl curtsied.

"Thank you for showing me how to dance!" she said.

"Thank you for showing me what you know!" replied Adam rather sadly as he seemed to sense his meeting with this most delightful child was ending. The child of rejection and longing took a step back and then another and another, always facing Adam, drawing ever further away and being enveloped more and more into the darkness. She neither smiled nor did not smile but the look on her face was a bit ambiguous – a sort of neither here nor there sunset of an expression. Adam's heart well and truly broke and sank and anything else a person's heart does at such a wrenching time, for who can listen as swans pass with chiming wingbeat and not mourn as they fly out of earshot and who cannot feel the touch of lamentation when a best friend departs to foreign lands for a season?

The girl disappeared from view but Adam still heard her stepping back and back until he heard her turn and run off, *maybe back to her parents*, he thought. So Adam knelt alone on the floor. He breathed in heavily a few times through his nose where the girl had blown her very life. He looked down at the key of two keys, stroking the still warm metal and just thinking to a depth he had never thought before. Adam touched his cheek where the girl's hand had been minutes earlier and thought of her. All alone was Adam now, kneeling on a bare wooden floor with seemingly a vast, dark space around him. *"Who?"* he thought, *"is working the loom to weave these hours of wonder for me?"*

So Adam knelt alone and waited…

…and waited

…and waited

…for sometimes it is good to wait, even though Adam really had no choice but to. The long and silent pause was undoubtedly giving birth to something. Teri-An's words, "You're among friends!", hushed any fears.

Approaching lone footsteps could be faintly heard, way off to one side, walking calmly. Adam was glad, but, despite Teri-An's words, fought fear at the same time, and who could blame him? He did not look in the direction of the footsteps but only knelt, awaiting the inevitable contact. The steps came on and Adam found a crumb of comfort in the fact that they sounded female in gait. Not an eight-year-old girl this time but a woman no doubt. Adam never moved a muscle as he had now become fully used to being controlled as events unfolded. He looked at the key of two keys and wished his young guide was singing her lullaby of touch to him now.

The womanly walk slowed and slowed until whoever it was stood right in front of Adam. Adam still did not look up and did not need to, as the woman bent over and put her hands under his shoulders and slowly lifted him up and up. Adam smelled perfume. He stood slowly until she was holding him by his fingertips. A heartbeat later and Adam was looking down on a beautiful young woman of about twenty-five years of age. Gone was childhood – now young womanhood kept Adam company. But what utterly took Adam's breath clean away was the fact that she wore a wedding dress.

Oh yes, this was a bride in cascading white waterfalls of silk that flowed and fell, falling earthward in sacred near silence, hitting the floor in a froth of lace hemming. The gentle rustling of the dress made interruption by speech seem blasphemous. A garland adorned her auburn hair. This shout of auburn was nearly alive in its style and with enough shades of brown, gold and copper to colour a great many autumns. Large curls and smaller curls churned in harmony, rolling on and on in hair so long she could easily sit on it. But these encounters were never without oddity and the young lady, this young bride, this lovely yet lonely figure in soft auburn swirls and drapes of white, the most gorgeous example of the Architect's skill, although wearing a subtle smile, had her eyes closed all the while and did not speak. Her head was bowed slightly as if in greeting.

So Adam stood with his fingertips touching the tips of her upturned hands. Now she slid right up close to Adam and put her right arm around him under his arm and curled her left up and around the back of his neck while resting her head over his heart. Not exactly the correct pose for a dance or romantic embrace but a pose for something else. The two stood like this for a minute or two and Adam awaited the next occurrence, which didn't seem to arrive. Then he remembered and closed his eyes.

Down in his heart or up in his head, Adam knew not exactly where, but with his eyes tightly closed, nostrils full of womanly scent and arms full of warm auburn and white, Adam saw things.

The sight that presented itself to Adam was frightening and majestic, for suddenly he was in a cathedral. Tall and dusty, tall and echoing, long and adorned with stained glass parables which a blasting sun narrated effortlessly every day was this building of ancient grey praise.

Back in the bride's arms, Adam drew breath sharply. Her eyes remained closed.

A building of such scale had a chasm of space within and yet was filled to bursting with old world beauty. The arches and pillars, the sculptures and pews, the windows of colour and the resting places of nobility all made this building what it was. Adam found himself standing right at the back, staring down the aisle. In the distance, right down at the front, he saw two people – one sitting, one standing.

Whether he was controlled by an outside force or just himself, Adam walked towards the pair.

As he approached, Adam saw that the one sitting

was a young man dressed as well as any groom could be dressed. However, he sat with his head in his hands and wept solidly. The standing figure was a minister who bent over the weeping and tried to comfort he who would not and indeed could not be comforted. The sun smeared the cheery colours of stained glass comfort as best it could upon the tragic scene but to no avail. Numbness at the inability to step in and right this obvious wrong swept up and down Adam's heart. Nonetheless, he approached, stood for a moment, listening to the unique sound of silent sadness, perhaps the worst kind there is, then put his hand on the groom's back.

Immediately, the young man looked up and Adam saw youthful handsomeness stricken with the black plague of severe loss. Anger began to well in Adam's heart.

"Have you seen my love?" asked the groom, defeatedly.

Adam knew exactly who he was referring to and didn't know whether to tell or be silent, such was the pitiful sight sitting before him on the pew. Adam knew whatever answer he gave would make the matter worse so said nothing. The groom went back to sobbing.

Adam knelt beside the man and asked, "Who has done this? Who has spoiled this day for you?" But now it seemed Adam was separate from those present and was unable to interact. He stood up abruptly and spoke very loudly, not to the man but to anyone who would listen.

"I said who has done...?"

Adam's question spluttered to a halt as he was shocked to see the whole cathedral, every single pew, was now filled with wedding guests who had not been there moments before when he walked past. The silent and mass appearance frightened Adam greatly, causing him to gasp and stagger back a step or two, bumping into the altar behind him.

This sudden congregation did the occasion proud in such finery but then Adam looked again and saw all had heads bowed and stood statue silent. And it was this silence that was so very frightening. Such a throng yet motionless with a truly deafening silence that nearly had its own echo in the cathedral.

Adam turned and looked at the altar. There sat the scroll. This time it was unfurled slightly and a few words could be read. Adam could see the words "Reason" and "Softness", which only intrigued him all the more. He tried to unfurl the tantalising parchment but it would not budge despite Adam's brute force. Again, it would seem, interaction with people and things was denied him.

He now whipped around at the sound of mass shuffling to see every person from one side of the cathedral move in orderly fashion and file out of the building. Adam ran to the departing and tried to halt one of them, asking, "Who has done this? Who has spoiled this day?", but she was supernaturally unstoppable and kept calmly walking. Adam felt her solid to the touch like stone and without give either in form or movement. He put himself between another and another, all the while shouting "WHO HAS DONE THIS? WHO HAS DONE THIS?", but he was effortlessly brushed aside, finally falling backwards on to the floor. The last of them disappeared out the door, leaving the cathedral filled in the most lopsided way.

Adam now threw all caution to the wind, stood up quickly and ran back to the still sobbing groom. He knelt down beside him and tried to shake his now rock-solid form, shouting, "I HAVE SEEN HER! YES, YES, I HAVE SEEN YOUR LOVE!", but realised that, one way or another, he was pleading with someone he was forbidden from relating to, an other-worldly being who was beyond his reach. Adam knelt with one hand on the groom's shoulder and wept into his other. He repeated over and over and over, "I have seen your love, I have seen her."

Suddenly there was the most beautiful smell imaginable and the touch of warm auburn and white. Adam was back in the bride's arms. Both were kneeling in the darkness in a gentle spotlight. Adam could have knelt and held her forever but the bride rose to her feet, lifting Adam with her. Still with eyes closed, she put a hand under Adam's chin and raised his head more and more then, *WHOOSH*, she breathed a short sharp breath into Adam's nostrils.

And the second person went to live way down in Adam's heart.

At that exact moment Adam heard a definite

CLINK sound. He pulled the strange key from his pocket to see another key had disappeared, leaving one – one wonderful key. He smiled and looked at his new sublime friend. She stood in her uniqueness, sweetness and feminine completeness – eyes closed, head slightly bowed. And why *should* she open her eyes if not to see her handsome one? Why open your eyes at midnight when the moon has waned, clouds gather and there is nothing to see? Adam had seen the whole story in a few brief minutes.

He did the only thing he thought appropriate and took her delicate left hand in his right. It was extremely warm. He gently rubbed his thumb in a circular motion across her fingers then tenderly kissed her blank ring finger. Adam didn't look up and see but this action brought a fleeting, thankful smile to the girl's face. She stood for a few seconds then walked off in the same direction she had approached. Adam did not watch her but simply stood, narrow eyed, staring at the floor. Her footsteps faded for quite a while and then were gone.

Suddenly, with very few hurried footsteps that approached so quickly they gave Adam no chance to discern their direction or become afraid, Teri-An literally collided into Adam's arms, nearly toppling him off his feet. She hugged Adam very tightly and was obviously crying. Adam's joy at seeing a familiar face was tempered with her distraught state. He reciprocated her tight hug.

*"Teri-An, what's the **matter**?"* asked Adam

forcefully. But Teri-An just sobbed into Adam's chest, occasionally using a tissue to wipe her eyes and dab her nose. Her hug was that of a drowning woman. Adam kissed her jet black hair and wrapped his hand around the back of her head to pull it in very close under his chin, which she seemed to welcome. The contrast between this person and the one who had lovingly served and chatted with him earlier was both bewildering and frightening. His heart broke for her.

"Teri-An, what on Earth *is it?*"

A sputter then a sniff then a sob and a sob – she finally spoke. "A blank canvas was I, I didn't want much, I only awaited the sable's touch."

"I don't understand, Teri-An. Help *me* to see so I can help *you*." Adam was trying his best – he hoped Teri-An knew this. She increased her already tight embrace and continued, ever so sadly, finally speaking the words that, up till now, were mostly hidden on the scroll:

> *There is valid reason why I was not born,*
> *to some I was softness, to others, thorn.*

"But you *have* been born, Teri-An! See, you're here with me right now, and then some!" encouraged Adam, who was reminded of the day he had huddle-walked Dolores out of that hospital. Adam felt that he himself was the drowning one – drowning in a confusion of emotion. Teri-An was as driftwood unto him. But this driftwood was soaked in tears and slippery, and it was salt water indeed as that is what tears are. He knew Teri-An was baring her soul and felt honoured, for raising true trust in someone is the same as raising a child – it takes years of careful nurturing and the willingness to sacrifice time and then more time, but Adam and Teri-An had only met hours before. Every interaction in this world Adam found himself in, every relationship he had struck up with a person, was either a case of great acceleration or deceleration.

"You don't know what you've done for us (sniff) I don't think!" said Teri-An. Her arms were around Adam's neck and she hung like a pendant of love.

"I haven't done *anything*, Teri-An! I was on my way home from work and…"

"Oh, but you have, you have, you **have**! You are so so special to us and we love you!"

"Who is "Us" then, Teri-An?" asked Adam, gobsmacked at the mention of the word "Love" but appreciating it nonetheless.

Teri-An looked up into Adam's eyes. She gazed at him in a way that, up to now, she had not. She smiled through her tears, held an outstretched arm into the darkness, and shouted "*US!*"

With that, the light returned, the diners returned, the lovely atmosphere that had reached out and saved Adam from the storm returned. All of it – every single bit of it – Harlequins, yummy smells and all, came bouncing back.

With one amazing difference…

Chapter 6
An Olive Branch and a Gift

Now everyone, every single person, the young, old and middle aged, stood in a guard of honour easily 100 feet long and ten people deep, forming a natural corridor towards the strange door that, earlier, had opened to let light gush in. Everyone was applauding, everyone was cheering and all were in unison of their love for Adam – their beloved Adam! Adam gasped and took a step back in shock at this sight, for a second releasing his grip on Teri-An, who sniffed one more time then smiled with a laugh.

"Whaaat!" was all that was in Adam's vocabulary at this moment and maybe for the rest of his life. Teri-An hugged Adam from behind with such a look of satisfaction on her face. The noise of cheering was borderline deafening and over-the-line joyous. Adam turned round to face Teri-An and was utterly blown away to see not only the cheery waitress but also the Child of Three Keys, the bride and the old woman. Adam's eye went straight to his youngest friend who had held him steady just when he needed it. He was more than delighted to see her again.

"Hey, you!"

He bent down to cuddle her and she did not

disappoint him, immediately continuing her lullaby of touch. Down and down sank Adam till he was on his knees, his head cradled by the child. Painfully, Adam found himself crying again, his tears soaking the front of her beautiful dress. His young friend had her eyes closed as if asleep. Adam wanted to say, "Thank you", over and over but was in no fit state to. The two knelt in unusual warmth.

But then, was this perfume? Was this sacred auburn and virgin white? The bride now knelt and cuddled Adam also. Now three knelt in unusual warmth.

Teri-An was next. The first friend Adam had made in this wonderful and frightening place knelt behind him and slid her arms under Adam's and hugged him, pressing the side of her head against his back. She was crying also. In the midst of mass cheering, in the midst of mass celebration, in the midst of this place in the midst of a storm in the midst of the Architect's love, Adam knelt in the midst as four knelt and huddled and cuddled in unusual warmth.

Finally, Adam felt a tender stroke to his cheek. The old woman had returned and now filled the remaining gap. All compass points were now accounted for, making it impossible for Adam's heart to flee in any direction. He just had to kneel there and be loved.

Well, what flooded Adam's heart now?

Requited love was the answer. Requited in all its forms – the visual and the unseen, the spoken and unspoken, that which was felt and never felt – that was what flooded Adam's heart now. No interruption or impediment spoiled this moment. Was Adam back in the womb? To the naked eye it appeared so. Was Adam being reformed into another creature? To the perceptive heart it appeared so. Adam was encased in love by the four stations of life who spoke a language others, up till now, had forbidden them to. They had silently told Adam their secrets and had imparted to him their woes. They had – because of Adam – been finally able to put down such heavy, thorny, hurting yokes and instead take up and wear the victory garlands of acknowledgement, for, in their world, acknowledgement is the costliest of treasures, more costly than a mighty blinding of pearls and bearing the price tag of a death.

Yes, Adam, you have wandered into a wonderful but solemn world. You are an amateur here, my friend. Those around you at this moment are here because they were forced to be here but note their joy, Adam. They know where you are from. You have seen things they longed to see but did not see. They desired to walk up and down where you have walked up and down but were forbidden from doing so. Their names are missing from your world but was jealousy your dining companion tonight, Adam? Did resentment meet you at the door, smile for you, take your coat and hand you that pretty menu? And who applauds you now? Not hatred, surely, would you not agree, Adam?

And who exactly is kneeling and holding you now? Be assured, if you needed them to kneel and hold you for eternity they would do just that. Yes, Adam, you may be a gentleman, you may have chivalrous moments that thrill your beloved Dolores, you may be gallant on occasion and be a rare, genuine "nice guy", but here you are a helpless babe in these matters, being held by people who have suffered the ultimate hammer blow to their destinies yet regard you in truest love. You – who have lost nothing – being held securely by those who lost all.

So the full compass of love meets the applause of Adam's many new friends. Two entities that, until Adam's visit, had never had opportunity to collide, now finally embrace. And what happens in such a situation? Birth is what happens – birth on many levels.

The four ladies slowly rose together, leaving Adam lying in a tight foetal position. They stood and stood. Then gestation was complete. Adam stretched and staggered to his feet as if he had slumbered for a number of months. He now stood without a single tear or red eye, he stood knowing the mystery, he stood knowing how it was in the collective hearts of all present. Indeed, Adam stood anew. Oh yes, he was the same old Adam – gallant on occasion, silly to order if it made Dolores laugh and putting off doing repair jobs around the house as long as possible – but now a new Adam also lived and breathed.

Teri-An ever so slightly smiled and put her hand on Adam's cheek. "You have to go home now, Sir."

"I don't want to, Teri-An," said Adam, emphatically.

"I know," she replied, "we…know and are so glad you say that but, as it stands, there is still much of your heart in your world and we would never take you away from that. You are just young and must enjoy what is rightfully yours – every day."

The two of them embraced. What a friend Teri-An was, what a caring soul Teri-An was, what a magnificent all-rounder of a citizen and woman Teri-An would have been. Loads of friends, starting with Dolores, would have been her witnesses to this. Teri-An, ostracised and knowing exactly what that word means. In times and places either behind or before, at some gathering, a gap, a space, a blank moment would ever so momentarily open up that Teri-An would have filled. If a smile ever flits across the face for no reason, it is because Teri-An would have put it there had she the chance. Somewhere, way off in another place, swans flew past with chiming wingbeat and someone's friend made ready to depart to foreign lands for a season.

"(sniff) Look, you've got me crying again!" said the cheery waitress.

"Can't I stay just an hour or two more?" asked Adam, feebly. He so wanted to smash every clock in the world if it would halt time.

"Here is your coat, Sir!"

She helped Adam on with his coat, fixed the collar and buttoned him up, motherly style. Suddenly, Adam remembered. "I never did read those words around the table edge."

"That's because they were not written for you. They were written for those to whom you will tell of this evening."

"You want me to tell others? I was going to do that anyway, Teri-An!"

"Yes, but you would have naturally told only a few across years to come. We want you to tell the world. We want you to tell those whose hearts ache because of us. For some reason a bridge opened up from you to us and you have crossed that bridge. You have done, said or thought something that was picked up on by the Architect, who saw fit to allow your visit. I have heard about this happening before, no doubt it will happen again. Write all this down and let them read. You came to us a bewildered traveller; we return you as our olive branch to the heartbroken. You worry about those words around the table; the Architect will make sure your story contains them all."

At this point, the door opened and the light shone in once again. Adam turned his head slightly and gazed straight into it but was in no way afraid. He turned fully to face it and step towards it.

"Just a moment, Sir, we have a gift for you!" said Teri-An, causing Adam to look back over his shoulder. Teri-An was gathered in a tight huddle with the Child of Three Keys, the bride and the old woman. They were looking down at something they held between them. Then Teri-An turned around very slowly and carefully. She was holding a baby wrapped in softness. No sooner did Adam register what he beheld but Teri-An placed the suckling into his arms. Adam stood wide eyed and wide mouthed, staring down at the newborn who looked up at him, hoping for love and ready to give a lifetime of it.

"*It's a girl, and she's all yours!*" said Teri-An, with such satisfaction in her voice. All Adam could do was give Teri-An a hopeless, helpless, ambiguous stare. He looked upon the baby, he looked upon his daughter.

"The Architect allows us to do this at our discretion, should a deserving case come along," Teri-An continued. "This plump little sweetling of a girl is yours completely. Behold, she comes to you and your wife with this wonderful twist: those who hear or read your story of this evening are at perfect liberty to view this baby as a down payment, an unbreakable promise and a cast iron guarantee from the Architect that their own sweetling is safe and sound just beyond the Door to Light. They are to think no more that they have done something that cannot be forgiven, for they have not! This is partly, and, at the same time wholly, why she has been gifted to you."

When you are with the object of your affections, it is enough to simply gaze, isn't it? You look, bewitched and hypnotised, frozen in ecstasy, delirious with the moment and anticipation of the next. Your feelings for that person have lain in an old cobwebbed chest, but now the chest has been found, the lock is gone and the lid lifts. You plunge your frostbitten, lonely hands within, deep down into the treasures of love. They are warm and golden. The warm coins jostle and clink excitedly in your heart as you stir and stir. Oh, now you are indeed wealthy! You laugh and wonder

"Just how good can it get? Why did I never feel this way before?" You see, those treasures were there all along. You carried them around for years without knowing – and only awaited the right person to show you where they lay.

And now, for sure, Adam knew where they lay. Teri-An stroked the baby's cheek with her finger.

"Hold her close, she wants to tell you something!"

So Adam put his face up to his daughter's, expectantly. The baby suddenly sneezed up into Adam's nostrils.

And the third and final person went to live in Adam's heart.

He did not need to look or feel with his hand but fully knew that the third key was now gone. Adam had been right all along – the Key of Three Keys cannot open just any lock. A heart in which a person sits, alone, on a plain wooden chair in the vastness was the lock the Key of Three Keys was designed for. Such a person was Dolores, among many, many others. This helpless infant would reach forth from tussled swaddling and comfort Adam's wife, wiping tears from both face and history. Oh, how bright the future was now!

And so the time had finally come. Adam again turned to face the bright doorway and stepped forward, carrying his daughter, along the guard of honour. People cheered and stepped out to hug Adam and kiss him. Party poppers, just like in Adam's world, burst forth with happy colour. Streamers soared and sparklers were waved. Confetti flew with abandon. Why was Adam's world not more like this?, is a question anyone would ask.

The door was reached now. A sun's worth of brightness, one inch away, shone, ready to engulf Adam. He turned for one last look at a sight he knew he might not see again. Faithful Teri-An stood beside.

"Will I see you again, Teri-An?"

"With all my heart I want to, but let's just wait and see," came her ambiguous reply, along with a barely perceptible smile.

"I want you to meet Dolores."

She reached up and pulled Adam's head right down to her level, whispering, "How odd we should see each other like this!" She kissed Adam on his cheek. He turned and took that final step.

Light became all, engulfing the world.

Chapter 7
Discharge and Home!

Adam sat in his car on his way home from work. The car was stationary. Everything was as it was one second before he encountered the storm. He sat, staring at the steering wheel. In his mind were thoughts of this and that. To look at him you would not initially think he had just been through an all-out unforgettable experience, such was the calm look on his face. Those thoughts went on about his mind – the working day, Dolores and the rom com, delicious soup, strange keys and cathedrals…wait…soup, keys and *cathedrals?* His look became a touch perplexed now.

Suddenly a lorry drove past, honking its horn and snapping him back to now. He realised he was stationary but without warning lights flashing or even an indicator. Starting up, Adam checked his rear view before moving on and saw all glory just behind him. He spun around violently in his seat. There in the back seat was the baby. Adam froze with sheer unbelief. What look on his face now? He hurriedly started the car and pulled off the road as far as he could get, hurriedly got out and threw open the back door. Yes, the baby really was there. He picked up the child. The action felt familiar and jogged strange memories just a little looser. Fresh was the suckling that hoped for love and was ready to give a lifetime of it. Adam kissed his daughter over and over. What need of wealth? What need of prestige? Nought were these weapons against the triumphing babe in arms! Then, realising the child was not his alone, Adam called the one person whose world would be truly upended by the helpless wrapped in a blanket.

"Hi…yeah, look…no, I'm fine…yeah, the storm… well, well…look, hang on. I'll be home soon…yeah, I'm on my way now and I'm bringing someone to meet you…we'll go another night ok? Love you too…bye!"

Now,
    at the end of it all,
        on a beautiful summer's evening,
            Adam drove home with his daughter.

Epilogue

It was not the night to be out.

Those brutal beasts, whose hoof prints are told of throughout antiquity, had not forgotten their promise to return and were now demanding serfdom from all. Unopposed in every whim, spoiled with subservience of all in their path, the blizzard stallions of winter galloped and guzzled the countryside with howls and deathly swirls.

In the midst of this white anguish there was a building, strangely untouched and strangely unworried by threats of war from the north. It was quite clear this was a restaurant, hinted at by the neon sign. The sign, as before, read TED, but then a few flickers and a fizz as the once broken sign that had been repaired came fully to life. It now read properly. It now read:

THE ABORTED

Once inside, a visitor would not encounter a waitress named Teri-An, for Teri-An was gone. She had, on some lovely and random evening, hearkened to a knock on the Door to Light and stepped through without fear. The cheery waitress now lived eternally in a land where blank canvas *always* meets sable and where being cheery is easy.

And outside,
   high up on a branch
    festooned with talon marks,
      an owl sat and gazed and thought...

And inside,
  beautifully,
    most beautifully,
      a piano played.

For Adam acknowledged what others would not
And Adam remembered what others forgot:
The Child of Three Keys, the one they dismissed
And the forsaken bride, whose hand Adam kissed
The waitress of Joy, whom heartache had felled
Was the one Adam cuddled and the one Adam held
And the sudden old woman, the last in life's line
Was the first to kiss Adam

Fox, Spider and Child, no longer to roam
Formerly outcasts, now having a home!
Whether ugly or handsome, whether softness or thorn
Escaped winter stallions and now were re-born
For in Adam's heart lay the Green Fields of Life
That won him a child to take home to his wife
And the cuddly baby, the first in life's line
Was the last to kiss Adam

Try not to despair over what you once did
Your baby is safe, although it be hid
Did you see how those diners took Adam to heart?
They'd do it for you if you took his part!
Let the words round the table answer your prayer
Go to it and find them for they really are there!
So keep your lullabies safe, don't throw them away
You'll have someone to sing them to on that great day
When you stand there with Adam!

The Explanation

In this explanation, none of the important points are the writer's own opinions. All points made are from the Bible (with which the writer agrees) and, as such, cannot be argued with. The writer's own opinions are kept solely to pointing out plot metaphors, twists etc.

Please read this explanation with a Bible to hand.

***

Dinner at Ted's is a Jesus centred story [1].

It is also a child centred story, dealing with both abortion regret and the loss of a child or children, not only children in the womb as with abortion or miscarriage but also older children. The main subject of the story is abortion and the regret of abortion. The fact that elements of the story can be applied to *any* kind of child loss is not accidental neither is it a coincidental "by product" of the story that it can be viewed in such a way. Loss is loss and the Bible has much to say to *any* parent beside themselves with grief over a lost child. If you have lost someone in their childhood for *any* reason then this story and all scripture references is *completely for you.*

This last point cannot be stressed enough.

No names in the story are without significance:

THE ARCHITECT [2] is God as you may have assumed.

HE WHO STANDS AT THE DOOR AND KNOCKS [3] is Jesus Christ. Notice that Jesus knocks but does not open the door. Those inside the door must open it.

ADAM [4] the main character, is so called because he represents all mankind, to which salvation through Jesus Christ is offered. The main protagonist is also a man as, in the emotive issue of abortion and other life issues considered "emotive", while having a female protagonist, it must be stressed, would have been entirely appropriate, men are all too often overlooked, along with would have been grandparents, would have been brothers and sisters and others classed as "would have beens". The good news of this little story applies just as much to these "would have beens", who also thirst for comfort.

DOLORES is from the Latin "Dolorem" meaning "Sorrowful". Adam's wife is so called as she has suffered repeated heartache at not conceiving a child. Carrying sore pangs of a longing for motherhood that remains perpetually unfulfilled, Dolores truly "Sits on a plain wooden chair, alone in the vastness". She represents all women who have had physical motherhood taken away from them due to the loss of a child.

TERI-AN is a waitress at the restaurant. Her normal disposition is cheery and caring. This side of her personality, however, hides heartbreak she carries around with her.

SAMUEL is one of the child patrons of the restaurant. He is named after the book of Samuel in the Old Testament. A happy and carefree child, Samuel runs and laughs with other children in unrestrained play. When asked, he teases Teri-An that he is more than one age, although it is never revealed exactly how old Samuel is.

***

The theme of the story is biblical forgiveness [5] coupled with restoration [6].

In the case of abortion regret, this forgiveness is for an act which was thought to be unforgivable; thought to be unforgivable in the eyes of God primarily and also in the eyes of the woman who is convinced that – by doing what she has done – she has put herself beyond the reach of God's grace and mercy [7].

The woman who has had an abortion and regretted it is distraught at what has been done and may harbour thoughts that any hope of a future with the child has been permanently forfeited as just recompense for her actions. She accepts this as her self imposed lot in life, only adding to the heartbreak she already endures.

Any parent who has lost a child is in a similar situation; facing an un-solvable equation of grief to which there is apparently no answer. They sit on a plain wooden chair, alone in the vastness, wishing there was an answer to their anguish; a key of some sort to unlock the enigma and bestow peace to mind and heart and grant their dream come true of being with their child again.

The key they seek comes in the form of forgiveness that is obtained by salvation through Jesus Christ [8]. No other way exists [9].

The "Key of Three Keys" represents this salvation through Jesus Christ. The key (salvation) only comes in to existence by the shedding of innocent blood caused by thorns piercing skin [10]; a sight Adam witnesses to his horror. Nothing Adam says or does causes the Key of Three Keys to come in to existence as it is the Architect (God) who creates it out of his love for Adam (mankind) [11].

When he is shown the Key by the Child of Three Keys, Adam is offered this salvation and reaches out and accepts it. This accepting paves the way for all subsequent events and blessings.

When the girl, the bride and Adam's own baby daughter breathe in to Adam's nostrils [12]; the Father, Son and Holy Ghost go to live in Adam's heart, again symbolic of the new birth.

Adam departs through the door to light upon which Jesus knocks earlier in the story; another symbol of the new birth. He returns to his world truly born again and holding in his arms that which he thought he would never hold.

***

In chapter 4, Teri-An is talking to Adam when a little boy called Samuel runs past. Teri-An calls to him by saying "C'mere a second, Samuel honey!" This "second, Samuel" is a reference to 2nd Samuel as found in the Old Testament. Samuel playfully tells Teri-An that he is both 12 and 23. Second Samuel 12:23 states:

" . . . I shall go to him, but he shall not return to me."

These words were spoken by King David who had lost his little boy through his own stupidity but now had the assurance that his son was alive and well in Heaven and that he would one day join him there.

Teri-An states: "Here, children differ slightly from us adults in that there is more than one way they can arrive". This is again referencing Samuel 12:23 in that it is not only children who are aborted who go to Heaven but also children who die from miscarriage, cot death, illness, accident or violence towards them [13]. King David's child did not die in the womb but in infancy.

This is very important for any grieving parent to know.

***

As Adam obtained salvation through Jesus Christ, so must you, if not already done. Simply say out loud from your heart:

"Dear God,

I come to you in the name of the Lord Jesus Christ. I realise that no amount of good works would ever qualify me for Heaven. Only by accepting Christ's substitutionary sacrifice at Calvary can I ever come in to right relationship with you. I now accept Jesus Christ as my Saviour and confess Him as my Lord. I am now truly born again, my name is written in the Lamb's book of life and Heaven is my home!

Thank you God!"

Adam did nothing to earn his salvation. It was manufactured on his behalf then offered to him. We do nothing to earn our salvation either. It was purchased for us by Jesus who was punished in our stead, leaving us to simply accept that act by accepting Jesus as Saviour [14].

What Adam *did* earn, however, was his visit to the restaurant...

Earlier in the story, we see Adam broken hearted at the loss of "the poor unborn sparrow" and also lamenting the worldwide unnoticed passing of the day on which it died. He acknowledges both the sparrow and the day itself as having individual significance and laments the world's "throwaway" attitude to such things. This does not go unnoticed by an omniscient Architect (God) [15] and Adam's visit to the restaurant is granted.

The restaurant is patronised by those who were not acknowledged by Adam's world; their status of being actual "people" not being recognised. Their time on Earth was slain, before it even began, by the sword of disregard.

During the visit, four of the patrons perceive Adam's loving heart and unhesitatingly pour out their sorrows to him. They drink their fill from the sweet oasis of Adam's consideration and quench their thirst for – at long last – acknowledgement. They love Adam deeply for acknowledging them as actual *people*; worthy of consideration, time and love. This appreciation is echoed by all present. All patrons know where Adam is from and also know he and his wife are childless. Exercising their right to discretion bestowed on them by the Architect, they reward Adam with a baby to take home and love.

Adam's attitude of heart symbolises the repentant heart of a woman who regrets an abortion [16]. The love Adam is shown by the Architect granting the visit symbolises God's abundant willingness to forgive such a woman hurting with abortion regret [17] and, it should be noted, to also forgive any who were party to the act but are now contrite about their involvement. The blood of Jesus covers all sins.

***

Twice during his visit, Adam is told:

"How odd that we should see each other like this!"

These words hint that those he interacts with know something Adam doesn't as yet. That "something" is that the baby he has been gifted is all the four people who poured out their hearts to him. Yes, it was . . .

Adam's own daughter who gave him the Key of Three Keys.

Adam's own daughter who stood before him in her wedding dress.

Adam's own daughter who served him in the restaurant, and . . .

Adam's own daughter whom he met as an elderly lady.

In time and as future years arrive, Adam's heart will be thrilled as he realises that the girl he and Dolores have is none other than Teri-An! He has seen Teri-An at the key stages of her life, including being the same age as himself and old age. Adam now understands the words "How odd we should see each other like this!" for what parent sees his child the same age as himself and what parent sees his child very elderly?

It is very important to note that Adam receives the Key of Three Keys (salvation) first and the baby second. This is because the only way for a bereft parent to go to their child is to first accept Jesus as Saviour.

***

At the beginning of this explanation we mentioned a much sought after but seemingly elusive forgiveness.

The "odd looking and very costly key" that represents salvation through Jesus Christ was offered to you the moment you picked up this book. If you needed to pray the sinner's prayer given and have accepted Jesus as your Saviour then, like Adam, you reached out and took the Key of Three Keys.

You are now forgiven, truly born again and the following scripture applies to you . . .

"Now therefore ye are no more strangers and foreigners, but fellow citizens with the saints, and of the household of God;" Ephesians 2:19

You are now a new creature in Christ Jesus [18] and, like Adam "stood anew" so you "stand anew" in right relationship with God! Your sins – including abortion(s) – have been wiped from the record. God himself – the all knowing – all present – all powerful creator of the universe – who can never ever make a single mistake, has no memory of any wrong you have done! [19].

Now you know, that despite doing what you did, you were still *well within* the reach of God's mercy and forgiveness! [20].

It is now for *you* to put *yourself* well within the reach of your *own* "mercy and forgiveness" concerning abortion. Forgive yourself and forgive yourself *completely*.

Now you know that, whether your child lost its life due to abortion, miscarriage or any of the evils of this world, they have been safe and sound in Heaven *all along!* Your child never stopped being yours in the sense of your love and relationship of course but what has been regained for you by Jesus is to go to be in the direct presence of that person. Your child has been returned to you in their tangible and huggable form!

With that forgiveness a tremendous burden is lifted completely. You can now journey on through life, and, when your time on earth is over, a truly fantastic reunion with your child can be anticipated! You will hold in your arms that which you thought you would never hold, either again or for the very first time! Like Adam, who knew "for sure" where his treasure lay, so you also know for sure where your child and "would have been" brother, sister, grandchild is! [21]

There was a truth you needed to hear [22]. As you read on through this book, you hoped that truth would also be the truth you so desperately *wanted* to hear, didn't you?

Now you know it was!

And just like Jesus said it would, the truth, now known, has set you free! [23]

Where is the "plain wooden chair" now? Look around you. It is gone! [24]

Knowing that, because of Jesus, all eternal calamity has now been successfully reversed and you will hold your child in your arms – for all time – you are free to look forward to your dying day with relish [25] and "Joy unspeakable!! [26]

***

The subtitle of this story is "An Olive Branch"

An olive branch is the symbol of peace. The offering of an olive branch by one person to another indicates that peace between two formerly at odds parties is sought for. The one offering the branch is happy to forget any differences entirely and hopes to rekindle friendship by the former opponent accepting said branch.

Genesis 8:11 reads:

"And the dove came in to him in the evening; and, lo, in her mouth was an olive leaf pluckt off: so Noah knew that the waters were abated from off the Earth."

It can be seen here that, after the global flood which wiped out all not in the ark, the humble olive leaf was the very first sign that peace and safety had returned. In Noah's hand, one little leaf was looked on as an entire world of peace; the whole spectrum of love and friendship being contained in one tiny piece of foliage. As Adam's entire world was "slammed to a halt by one tiny bird's egg" so too, no doubt, Noah's world stood still for a while as he gazed at that which, ordinarily, would be swept aside and forgotten.

Long ago, literal branches were indeed given at times to hopefully bring reconciliation. Today, these "olive branches" are more metaphorical than anything. They usually take the form of a friendship card accompanied by a bunch of flowers or chocolates. Other "branches" can be a phone call or a nervous knock on your door or even a simple smile when you next meet that person. Maybe you have received a few or given out a few. Most of us have been there.

"Dinner at Ted's" is an olive branch from the baby you aborted to you. In the story we come to see that all in the restaurant know exactly where Adam (you) is from, yet all they wish to give Adam (you) is love; they being incapable, and unwilling, of anything else.

Your broken and repentant heart has been seen from a mile away by God who, like the father of the prodigal son, rushes with all his might to flood your world with forgiveness as Noah's world was flooded with water.

Out of both those biblical floods comes one thing only
. . . peace.

Now
at the end of it all
as you sit there reading and crying
your child is yours once more!

Scripture References

This list is far from exhaustive. Any reference Bible will point you to other scriptures on the specific area of interest.

1. Ps 118:22
   Col 1:17,18
   Rev 22:13

2. Job 38: 4,5
   Heb 3:4
   Heb 11:10

3. Rev 3:20

4. 1st Cor 15:22

5. Isa 1:18
   John 3:16
   Heb 8:12

6. Isa 25:8
   1st Thess 4: 13 – 18
   Rev 21: 4

7. Luke 15:21

8. John 3:3
   Rom 10:9 – 13

9. John 14:6
   Acts 4:12

10. Isa 53:7
    John 19:2
    Acts 3:14
    1st Peter 3:18

11. Luke 2:11
    John 3:16
    1st John 4:10

12. Gen 2:7

13. Mat 18:3 & 19:14   14. Eph 2:8,9

15. Mat 10:29   16. Ps 51:17
                             Mat 12:20

17. Ps 103:12   18. 2nd Cor 5:17
    Isa 1:18
    1st John 1:9

19. Rom 11:27   20. Num 11:23
    Heb 8:12   Isa 50:2 & 59:1

21. Mat 6:21   22. 2nd Sam 7:28
                           John 17:17

23. John 8:32 & 36   24. 1st Cor 15:55
    Rom 6:18

25. 2nd Cor 5:1   26. 1st Peter 1:8

Afterword

Dear Friend,

I hope you enjoyed reading "Dinner at Ted's".

Like all stories, I suppose, it can be read on several levels and enjoyed in different ways.

If you simply looked on it as an entertaining way to pass an hour or so, then I am so glad you came along for the ride! It was great fun to meet you and become acquainted, it really was!

I hope to see you again – and soon!

But, if the story has touched you on a way deeper level and maybe even made you cry, then you surely see "Dinner at Ted's" as an antidote for the pain you feel concerning the subject matter, don't you?

Be in no doubt then that this story contains real and concrete truths that will, if embraced, help lift the burden you have carried.

Because, you see, truths are exactly that – truths!

And, as somebody once said:

"You shall know the truth
            and the truth will make you free."

Your new friend this day,

Edward, St David's

P.S.

Q: But what about Teri-An? I thought no names were without significance.

A: Well, if you take the name "Teri-An" and rearrange the letters, you get the French word "Naitre" which means . . .

"To be born!"

For more information on Edward, St. David's
and future releases please go to:

www.edwardstdavids.com